NEED ME

CYNTHIA EDEN

For my readers…thank you so much for your support! And I sure hope that you enjoy Dev's book.

CHAPTER ONE

"Please. I'll pay any price. I just—I don't want to die." Julianna Patrice McNall-Smith clenched her hands into fists as she was led into Devlin Shade's office at VJS Protection, Inc.

The company was high-end, supposedly very discreet. If you had a problem, VJS was the solution. They offered protection. A twenty-four hour, seven-days-a-week bodyguard service, and with the way her life was falling straight to hell, she could sure use that service.

"Why don't you sit down?" Devlin said, his deep voice rumbling as he closed the door behind her, sealing them inside the sanctuary of his office.

She probably shouldn't like his voice as much as she did. She shouldn't be so aware of him. It was wrong.

So why did he feel so right?

Julianna sat down and carefully crossed her legs in front of her. She noticed that Devlin's gaze dipped to her legs, and she tensed for a moment. *Stop it. Keep your mask in place. You can do this.*

He pulled his stare away and paced toward his desk. He didn't sit down, though. Instead, he propped his hip against the edge of the desk and stared at her.

"My lawyer told me to come to you," Julianna said because she didn't like the way silence stretched in that office. "Sophie Sarantos said your firm was good at discreet protection." But her laugh was brittle. "I don't really care if you're discreet or not. I just need help." Because Julianna knew a killer was out there, and she didn't particularly want to die.

Not when I've just started living again.

"I'm well acquainted with Sophie," Devlin said.

His voice was really quite dangerous. So rumbly and deep. It made her think of things she had no business even considering right then. Julianna straightened her shoulders. Maybe he wasn't jumping to take the job because of the things he'd heard about her. "I'm not a killer."

He just stared back at her. His eyes were such a bright, brilliant blue. Gorgeous eyes. When she looked into his stare, Julianna felt a little bit lost — and she knew that could be a dangerous thing. Devlin was tall, strong, with powerful, wide shoulders that stretched his suit jacket. His thick, dark hair slid away from his forehead. Devlin was a handsome man, not perfectly so, but handsome in a rough, rugged way. His cheeks were sharp, his jaw cut and square, his nose was a little bit hawkish, but that just added to his rugged air. And his lips…

I have no business noticing his lips.

She shifted a bit in her seat and uncrossed her legs. Then, nervously, she re-crossed them immediately. Her skirt slid against her skin.

Devlin cleared his throat. "Your case is going to be delayed. You realize that, of course. With the prosecuting ADA now dead — and with all the news that the guy was a straight-up psycho who'd been stalking *your* lawyer, hell, there's no way you'll be seeing the inside of a courtroom anytime soon. All of ADA Eastbridge's cases are about to come under one hell of a scrutiny. All those people that he sent to prison — they'll be shouting injustice and demanding new trials. Because of him, the prosecutor's office is a serious cluster fuck right now." He waited a beat. "And that can only be good for you."

Her breath felt cold in her lungs. "Good for me? Sophie isn't just my lawyer. She's also my friend. That man — Clark Eastbridge tried to kill her! That is hardly good for me."

Devlin watched her with that unreadable stare of his.

"You mean it's good for me…" She understood now. "Because Clark Eastbridge being a psychotic prick means I probably won't see the inside of a jail." Sophie had actually told her the same thing. Eastbridge had been pursuing her case with particular fury, and now that the truth about him was out...well...even the press was going a bit easier on her.

"That's exactly what I mean. Guilty or innocent, things have changed for you now."

She shot to her feet and nearly leapt toward him. Their legs brushed as she leaned in toward him. "I'm not guilty."

He shrugged. "I'm not on your jury, so it's not my place to say."

His words hurt her. Why she should be surprised he thought she was a killer, Julianna didn't know. Plenty of people had thought and *said* the same thing. That she was a calculating woman who'd taken herself a rich husband. She'd bided her time until she was legally set with his money, then she'd brutally killed him.

If only people knew the truth about her dead husband.

If only they knew the truth about me.

"Until the real killer is caught, I do have to worry about the possibility of spending the rest of my life in jail." And that couldn't happen. She'd already lived too long in a cage. She wouldn't be doing it again. Even Sophie didn't know that Julianna had made plans...escape plans. If things started to look too dark, she was going to vanish.

And, lately, with fear crowding ever closer, vanishing had started to look like the perfect choice. *I just don't want the world to remember me as a killer.*

"You want me to catch the *real* killer?" Devlin asked, cocking his head a bit as he stared down at her.

Her hands lifted and curled around his shoulders. Why was she touching him? Julianna wasn't sure, but she just tightened her hold on him. "No, I want you to keep me alive. He's after me. I know he is, and I want to hire you as my bodyguard." Money wasn't an issue for her. Not anymore.

For just an instant, the past swam before her. That terrible morning when she'd woken on the floor of her den and found her husband's dead body right beside hers. His blood had soaked the carpet. It had been under her body. On her.

Everywhere.

Devlin's gaze slid over her face. Slowly. As if he were taking her in. Julianna was far too conscious of her fingers on his shoulders. Of his body so close to hers. Of —

"Do you always get what you want?"

Her brow furrowed.

"Do you always…" Devlin continued, voice roughening a bit, "use your body to get what you want?"

Her mouth dropped open in shock, then immediately closed as rage swept through her. "I'm not using my body." She jerked away from him. Sophie had been so wrong about the guy. Going to Devlin had been a huge mistake. He wasn't the man she'd thought, not at all.

Julianna rushed for the door, but Devlin caught her before she'd taken more than a few steps. He curled his fingers around her shoulder and spun her back to face him. "Every news story says that you're a femme fatale. The woman who seduced billionaire Jeremy Smith and convinced him to marry her after a whirlwind courtship."

She was the one who'd been seduced. And trapped.

"And then you come in here, offering to pay *anything* if I help you."

Her chin shot up. "I was talking about money. Any amount you wanted. I wasn't talking about paying with myself." And she hurt right then. Why, Julianna didn't know. He wasn't the first person to hurl insults at her. "Despite what you might think, I'm not a whore, high-priced or otherwise."

His fingers slid down her arm. "My mistake."

"Yes," her voice had turned icy, "it was your mistake. But it was mine, too. I never should have come here. I'll find someone else." She gave him a curt nod. "Forget you ever saw me."

She turned on her heel and once more aimed for the door — and freedom.

"Forgetting you won't be easy," Devlin said. "No hope of that."

But she wasn't stopping now. He'd insulted her, attacked her…and she'd just wanted his help. He had no idea how afraid she was — every single moment — and she needed the fear to *stop*. She hadn't been able to sleep for a full night, not since before Jeremy's death. Her nerves were shattering, and the terror had to stop. Julianna grabbed the door knob, yanked that door open, and hurried outside.

"Julianna, wait!"

No way. *Mistake. Mistake. Mistake.* The word pounded through her head as she rushed for the elevator. But he was right behind her. She could hear his footsteps and her heart just raced harder in her chest. She jumped into the elevator and her fingers stabbed at the buttons.

Before the doors could close, he stepped inside with her.

That space was way too small for the two of them.

But the doors had *just* closed, and now they were alone in that elevator.

"You need to know," Devlin began. "When I take a case, I make it a point to learn every secret that my client may have. I never go into any situation blind. Not anymore. When you do that, deadly mistakes happen."

"You're not taking my case, so it hardly matters." She thought they'd already gotten that clear. "There are plenty of other bodyguards in the city. I'm sure they'll take my money without even thinking twice." *And* without digging into her past. She didn't want Devlin knowing her secrets. She didn't want anyone knowing them.

Why was the elevator so slow? She craned around him, trying to see the control panel.

"Why do you think someone's after you?"

Seriously? "Oh, I don't know…maybe because I woke up in a pool of my dead husband's blood. Someone drugged me and just left me there. And then, let's see, maybe it could be the emails I've been getting. Those lovely notes that say I won't get away with my crimes. That I'm next. Could be that," she muttered.

The elevator chimed. The doors opened. *Yes.* She was on the ground floor and home free.

"Julianna…"

She shook her head and marched through the lobby and out into the night. It was late, the street was pretty much deserted—and, lucky her— she'd gotten a parking spot just a little bit down the block.

Her heels clicked on the sidewalk. The cold wind caught her hair, tossing it behind her as she hurried. Going to VJS had been a colossal mistake. For the first time, Sophie had led her astray. Fumbling, Julianna pulled her car keys from her purse. Her fingers closed around them, and she remotely unlocked the car.

"Has anything else happened?"

She almost jumped at his voice. He was far, far too close.

And Devlin was reaching out to her again. Not roughly, but, carefully curling his hand around her.

"Julianna, *please*, just stop."

He'd rather gritted out the *please* request.

But she stopped. Her fingers slid over the keys. It was getting colder and she thought she even felt the light drop of snowflakes on her.

"Has anything else happened to make you think that you're in danger?" Devlin demanded.

Her finger pushed the button to start her car's ignition. The engine growled to life. She shook off Devlin's hold and turned to go—

Her top-of-the-line, way-too-expensive luxury car erupted into flames. A loud boom filled the air, making her ears instantly ring even as Julianna was tossed back, flying from the force of the blast. But she didn't fly far because Devlin grabbed her. He wrapped his arms around her and turned so that his body was shielding hers when they hit the ground.

She couldn't hear anything but the ringing in her ears. She could see Devlin's face. His mouth was moving but—

"Are you all right? Dammit, Julianna, talk to me!"

She could feel something wet sliding down her cheek. She knew it wasn't tears. She'd cried all of those out already. So it had to be blood.

"Julianna?"

"This…" Julianna managed to say. "This happened."

The furrow between his brows deepened.

Her fingers curled around his arms. "You asked…" Dear God, her car was *burning*. Well, what was left of it, anyway. "You asked what happened to make me think I was in danger…*This* happened."

Someone had just wired her car to blow. If she'd been in it, or, hell, maybe if she'd even been a few steps closer, Julianna knew she would have been dead.

"I'm taking your damn case," Devlin growled.

Good. Because she really wasn't in the mood to die.

CHAPTER TWO

"I hardly think that I need to stay at your place." Julianna's words were calm. Almost excruciatingly polite. She stood in his home, her hands folded in front of her, her clothes torn and dirty, and smeared blood was on her cheek. "I have a home where I can stay, you know. I don't need—"

"Until I can figure out more about your case," Devlin gritted out, "I want you staying with me."

A freaking car bomb. How the hell did that relate to the stabbing death of her husband? He'd felt the lance of that heat across his skin. Devlin knew just how damn close they'd both come to serious injury. Someone was definitely out to get Julianna, and if he hadn't thought she was innocent before, well, he was sure leaning that way now.

She looked vulnerable standing there. Delicate. Fragile.

And too beautiful by far.

Julianna was one of those women who seemed to have a perfect, untouchable beauty. Cheekbones made of glass. Skin creamy and smooth. A slightly curving chin, a button nose, but lips — lips that were full and sinful. Her lips were currently unpainted, but they'd been a slick red when she first walked into his office.

Too sexy.

Now the only red on her…that was the faint blood that smeared across one high cheekbone. She'd been cut during the explosion. He hated that she'd been hurt. Devlin pointed down the hallway. "You can use my bathroom to clean up." The cops had rushed to the scene. He and Julianna had been grilled, again and again. He'd actually gotten lucky because Detective Faith Chestang had been leading the investigation. That woman knew how to get shit done at the PD. She also knew to keep him in the loop on this investigation, just as VJS would be sure to keep her updated on all the intel they uncovered.

Julianna's head was tilted down. Some of her blonde hair had come loose from the twist at the back of her head. Those tendrils slid against her cheeks.

"Julianna?"

She glanced up at him and when he met her gaze, it was as if he'd just taken a punch to the gut. Julianna's eyes were so deep. A dark chocolate, but flecked with gold. Gorgeous eyes.

Eyes that seemed to see *into* him, and Devlin couldn't have that. He didn't want anyone seeing the particular sins he carried in his soul.

"Do you ever feel like…" Julianna began, her voice soft, "you're trapped in some kind of nightmare? And no matter what you do, you just can't wake up?"

He'd been there, a time or twenty. "Your nightmare started when you woke up to find your husband's dead body."

She laughed, the sound bitter and sharp. "No, the nightmare began after I said 'I do' to my husband. By then, it was too late."

Devlin tensed. He'd suspected this might have happened—and it fucking pissed him off. "He hurt you."

She turned away. Her steps were slow as she headed to the bathroom. "Let's just say I didn't exactly cry over his body."

"What did he do?"

She didn't answer. Julianna continued down the hall, presumably going to the bathroom. His eyes narrowed as he watched her. If he was taking her case—and he *was* – then he needed to know all the details of her marriage. Even if those details made him want to go out and kill Jeremy Smith. *You can't kill the dead.*

If only. Devlin turned and headed into his home office. The space was filled with top-of-the-line computers that would give him access to nearly everything. Early in life, he'd discovered his talent with computers. They'd opened doors for him. Shown him a whole new world.

A world of secrets and lies. People pretended so often, they hid their true selves, but with his computers, he could find their secrets.

Devlin sat down at his desk. In seconds, he'd pulled up the news stories about Julianna's trial.

Socialite charged in murder of developer husband.

Police arrest wife…charge her with the murder of billionaire Jeremy Smith.

She'd been tried quickly in the court of public opinion. After all, she'd been alone in the house with her husband. Her fingerprints had been on the knife. Her husband's blood had been found on her clothes.

And witnesses had come forward. Folks who'd been too willing to share that the gorgeous Julianna and her prominent husband hadn't exactly been living in wedded bliss. There had been stories of jealous rages. Arguments. A secret lover…Jeremy's step-daughter, Heather Aslo, had only been too happy to point her well-manicured finger at Julianna. She'd been sure that Julianna committed the crime.

Devlin leaned forward. He needed to access the police files on her case. So maybe he was bending — breaking? — the law a bit. His fingers flew over the keyboard. He'd get the information that he needed.

A soft hand touched his shoulder.

Swearing, he whirled around.

Julianna was there. Her face had been scrubbed clean of make-up. Her hair was wet, falling to her shoulders and brushing over the white, terry-cloth robe that she wore. His robe.

He hadn't even realized how much time had passed. When he started working, he tended to get lost and with this case —

"Digging up all my dirty secrets?"

He hadn't heard her walking across the room. He *should* have heard her. He glanced down, automatically, and saw her red toenails.

Were toes supposed to be sexy? Shit, but he had to get his act together with this woman. His gaze shot back to her face.

"You could ask me," Julianna continued, giving a slow shake of her head. "Instead of just digging and assuming that I'd lie to you."

Right. Just ask. "Who's your lover?"

She blinked at him.

She'd been beautiful with her makeup, it had given her a sophisticated, polished air. Without it, she looked more vulnerable, a bit younger...and still too sexy. Devlin realized that when Julianna was around, he thought with his dick far too much.

"I don't have a lover."

Lie. He sighed. "Come on. I thought you weren't going to lie."

"I'm not lying." Her hands slid into the pockets of the robe. "I don't have a lover."

"Your husband has been dead and buried for seven months—"

She flinched at that.

"And you haven't been with anyone since he died? A woman like you? You expect me to believe that?"

Julianna backed up a step. "A woman like me? Just what kind of woman am I?"

A woman who made him think of sin and silk sheets. Of soft moans and hot sex. He cleared his throat and very wisely decided not to tell her that. "Multiple witnesses reported that your husband believed you'd been having an affair. There were public arguments—"

"Right." She cut him off, her voice clipped. "There were plenty of arguments. Because if my dress was cut too low or if it was too tight, Jeremy thought I was trying to seduce every man in the room. If I went out for a jog and didn't come back within twenty minutes, he was sure I'd met a lover. He hired several PIs—but they all told him the same thing, I wasn't cheating."

He waited.

"I couldn't cheat, even if I'd wanted to. He was always watching or he always had someone watching me." Her face paled and her gaze seemed to see the past. "I'm not going to jail, because I've already been a prisoner. *His* prisoner. He controlled my life, and I *hated* him for it."

Devlin had suspected something like this. "He abused you."

Julianna's gaze sharpened on him. "That wouldn't make sense. He wanted me to be his perfect wife, perfect all the time. If I had bruises or broken bones, how could I be perfect?" There was something in her voice—a hitch—that made him think she was lying again.

He didn't want lies between them. "You hated him, so why didn't you leave him?" But Devlin already thought he knew the answer. Money. The number one motivator for—

"Stop it." Now anger bit in her voice. "You think I don't know what you're thinking?" Then she shot forward and jammed her finger into his chest. "You're thinking that I'm some slut who had her eyes on the prize. That I married Jeremy for his money and that I stayed with him—stayed in that hell—because I wanted the cash he'd give to me."

"That's a story I've heard before," he replied bluntly. She wouldn't be the first woman to make a trade like that. Not the first woman *or* man.

"It's not my story."

She still had her finger jabbing into his chest. He lifted a brow. "Why don't you tell me your story?"

"I thought I loved him."

Devlin's whole body tensed.

"What? You think I'm too mercenary for that? Too cold? It's the truth, okay? I was working for Jeremy, in his PR department. I didn't want to date the boss, I didn't want that kind of reputation, but he…courted me." Her finger slid away. Her shoulders rolled back as she straightened her spine. "And in the beginning, it was nice. Flowers. Dinners. He made me feel special. Like I mattered to him." Her smile was bittersweet. "I hadn't exactly felt that way a lot."

Why the fuck not?

"It was a whirlwind courtship and marriage. I should have slowed down. I should have played it safe. But I'd been playing things safe my whole life, and I took a chance." She shook her head. "I realized my mistake soon enough. When your husband starts screaming at you because you make the mistake of glancing at a handsome man on the street, you know something is wrong."

He waited. She didn't say anything else. "But you stayed…"

"He had power. Money."

Right. They were back to—

"He made sure I didn't have either. I had no access to our checking account or our savings account, and he had his flunkies transfer all of my own assets over to him the minute I said, 'I do'. I told you already, it got to the point where I couldn't go anywhere without him watching me—or without one of his guards there to follow my every step. I was his prisoner. Another acquisition that he'd wanted, and now that he had me, Jeremy had no intention of letting me go."

Anger and fear—he could see those emotions on her face and hear them in her voice. Devlin ran his hand across the stubble that lined his jaw. "I can't help you if you just lie to me."

She sucked in a sharp breath. The top of the robe parted a bit, revealing her creamy skin and the swell of her breasts. "I'm not lying!"

"Yes, you are." He jerked his thumb toward the computer. "One of the first things I did was access your medical reports."

She paled.

"Two days after your wedding, you broke your right wrist."

"I fell."

"It was shattered. According to the report, the injury was consistent with your wrist being slammed in a door."

Her long lashes flickered.

"Did you try to get away from him then?" Devlin asked, his own anger growing because of the pain that she'd been through. "You're a smart woman. I bet you were ready to cut and run once he dropped his charming mask, but something stopped you that day. *He* stopped you, right?"

"Is that what you want to hear?" Julianna turned from him and paced to the window. "That I realized I'd made a huge mistake? That I ran to my car, jumped inside and tried to get away from him?" Her soft sigh slipped back to him. "That Jeremy yanked me out of the car and when I fought him, he slammed the car door shut on my wrist?"

His hands fisted. Fury burned in his blood.

"Why the hell would I have stayed with him if he did that to me?" Julianna asked. "I would have run, money or no damn money."

He stalked toward her. "Maybe there was a reason you couldn't go."

She turned to look back at him.

"Tell me everything, Julianna. Tell me or I won't be able to do my job."

Her lower lip trembled, but she quickly pressed her lips together, stopping that tell-tale movement. Moments ticked by in silence.

"Tell me," Devlin urged again. There had to be something there. Yes, she'd hated her husband — that was obvious. Jeremy cutting off her money would have slowed her down, but if she wanted to get away…

"Sometimes, the only way out is death."

"No." Devlin was the one to reach out to her then, but he made sure to keep his grip gentle as his fingers curled around her shoulders. "There are other options. Death isn't an escape. It's just the easy way."

She laughed at him. "There's nothing easy about it."

His eyes narrowed on her. They were so close now. Close enough for him to easily see the gold flecks in her eyes. Close enough to kiss.

If he'd wanted to kiss her.

If she'd wanted to kiss him.

"What did he have on you?" Devlin murmured.

And there it was. Her pupils expanded. Her delicate nostrils flared. Devlin knew he'd struck gold. "He blackmailed you into staying with him, didn't he?" Devlin pushed. "You said it wasn't the money, so it had to be something else. *Tell me*. What did he have on you?"

"I'm done talking for tonight." She tried to pull away.

Keeping his hold gentle, but firm, he didn't let her go. "I'm not done with you. Tell me your secrets, Julianna…or I'll discover them on my own. After all, you're the one who said I should just ask you. I'm asking. Will you be telling?"

Her gaze searched his. He waited, wondering what she could have done that would have been so terrible that she'd stayed with that bastard. Stayed in his house and his bed and—

Julianna leaned toward him. She rose onto her tip toes, and she kissed him. He hadn't been expecting that move from her. He'd fantasized about it, sure, but Devlin hadn't anticipated she'd actually kiss him.

But he wasn't a fool. If Julianna wanted to kiss him, then who the hell was he to argue?

He leaned down, leaned *closer*, and put his arms around her. She was small, delicate, while he was the exact opposite. Devlin topped out at a few inches past six feet, and he was well aware of the strength in his body. Strength he used carefully, with her. Devlin picked her up, holding her easily and her mouth pulled back from his in surprise.

"What are you—" Julianna began.

"You started this," Devlin growled back. "I'll finish it." Then he pressed her back against the nearest wall. He held her there, easily, and he kissed her again.

Her lips were parted. Moist. And when his tongue stroked into her mouth, her taste made him feel a little drunk. Sweet but rich.

And she was kissing him back. Not hesitantly, but fully, moving her lips and her tongue against him, and Devlin's cock swelled against the front of his jeans. He didn't know what game she was playing right then, and he actually didn't care.

He just wanted her to keep playing it.

Her robe had come loose a bit at the top, and he wanted to shove that robe out of the way. He wanted to put his hands on her breasts and feel her nipples against his palms.

But he kept kissing her. Hot and hard. Thrusting his tongue past her lips, and when she arched toward him, desire pounded through his veins. Her legs rose and wrapped around his hips. Her nails sank into his upper arms. She pulled him closer, and closer was exactly where he wanted to be.

His mouth slid from hers, but only so he could kiss a hot path down her neck. She shivered against him. He used the edge of his teeth, lightly scoring her flesh. Was she completely naked beneath that robe? He was going to find out. He'd strip her and then—

"Stop."

Devlin blinked. He really, really hoped he'd misheard her.

But Julianna's hands were pushing at him now and her legs had slid away from his hips. "Let me go, now."

Jaw locking, he did. And Devlin stepped back so he wouldn't give in to the urge to grab her again and pick up exactly where he'd just left off.

Her cheeks were flushed. Her eyes glittered. "That was a mistake."

His spine shot up. "You're the one who kissed me." And he knew exactly why she'd done it. To stop his questions. To distract him.

Consider that a successful distraction. He didn't want to question her anymore. Fuck her? Most definitely, yes.

"It was *my* mistake." She edged away from him. Her hands quickly adjusted the robe for maximum coverage. "I didn't expect that."

Now she had made him curious. Eyes narrowing, cock aching, temper rising, Devlin asked, "What, exactly, didn't you expect?"

Her lashes lowered. She stopped adjusting the robe. "I didn't expect to want you that much, not from just a kiss."

Every muscle in his body locked down. "Baby, you should be careful saying things like that to me."

Her lashes lifted. Her gaze met his. "It was my mistake," she said again, and she turned for the door. "I won't be repeating it."

Oh, but I hope you do.

She stopped at the door, her hands on the wooden frame. "Where do I sleep tonight?'

"The guest room is down the hall. Third door on the left."

She nodded, but then she glanced back. "And where will you be?"

"I'll be in the room right—"

A hard pounding on his front door stopped Devlin's words. Frowning now, he hurried toward her. His penthouse was private—for a damn good reason. He wasn't the type to want uninvited visitors. And *no one* but his partners at VJS—Chance Valentine and Lex Jensen—were ever to be let up to his home without an announcement. His doormen knew that rule.

So who was pounding at his door?

"Devlin?" Julianna sounded worried. "You expecting someone?"

No, not that late. It was nearing midnight. Definitely not the time for any other guests—wanted or unwanted. Shaking his head, he hurried past her and went to the main door. He glanced through his peephole, and when he saw who was on the other side of the door, tension coiled in his body. Devlin opened the door.

Detective Faith Chestang stood on his threshold. She wore a no-nonsense suit, and her badge was clipped to her belt. Her hair was combed away from her face, and her determined expression said she meant business. Faith was an attractive woman, an African American in her early thirties, and a general force to be reckoned with.

"I tried to keep her downstairs, sir," Peter Close, the doorman said quickly, "but—"

Faith sighed, cutting through his words. "But I'm a cop and my badge gets me in all kinds of places." She lifted her dark brows. "It's about to get me inside this fancy penthouse of yours right now."

Devlin moved, blocking the entrance. "Unless you have some kind of warrant, it's not."

She smiled at him. He didn't know her as well as Chance did, but Chance had told him that Faith was a good cop, one he could trust.

Devlin didn't exactly trust many cops.

"I need to see Julianna," Faith said flatly.

"And you think she's here?"

Faith glanced over his shoulder. "Yes, I think she's about five feet behind you, wearing *your* robe." She gave a little whistle. "Cozy. I didn't expect that."

Swearing, Devlin whirled around. Sure enough, Julianna was there. What was up with the woman's silent moving? If he didn't know better, he would have thought she'd had some kind of special training. Chance and Lex both could take silent steps like that, to sneak up on their prey, but those guys were ex-military.

"I need you to come with me, Julianna," Faith said.

"Why?" Devlin's question, not Julianna's. Julianna hadn't moved.

"Because there's been another murder," Faith said, her delicate jaw hardening a bit. "And I'm afraid Julianna is tied to this one, too."

Devlin took a step back, clearing the path so that the cop could make direct eye contact with his new client.

Faith stared at Julianna. "People sure do have a habit of dying around you." Her gaze slanted to Devlin. "If I were you, I'd be very careful. Men who sleep with Julianna tend to wind up dead."

Julianna surged forward. "Who's the victim?"

Faith was watching her, the way a hungry spider might watch a fly. "Your lover."

Julianna told me she didn't have a lover.

"Th-that's not possible," Julianna said, her voice breaking. "I don't have a lover."

Faith gave her a long look. One that took in the robe Julianna was wearing and Julianna's swollen, red lips. "It looks to me like you may have more than one." Suspicion was in her drawl.

"I *don't*," Julianna hotly denied.

"That's not what the photographs say." Faith put her hands on her hips. "Now we can do this easy or hard. If you want me to lead you out in cuffs—again—I can do that."

"No." Julianna's voice was hushed. "Just, let me change, all right? I'll be right back." Then she turned and fled down the hallway.

Devlin didn't speak until she was gone. "Who is he," he asked, voice lethally soft, "and how did he die?"

Faith laughed, but the sound held no humor. "Seeing as how you're supposed to be so good at investigating, I would've thought that you'd do a little more research on your own lovers."

"She's not my lover." *Not yet.* But he sure wanted her.

Faith pointed at him. "Consider yourself lucky that I arrived. Men who fall for Julianna have a tendency to end up in a pool of blood."

Not the best visual. "Who is he?" Because Julianna had seemed so sincere when she'd told him that there was no one else.

Right before she'd kissed him.

What the hell? Am I going soft? Since when did he let a pair of warm, brown eyes trick him? Obviously, she'd been trying to seduce him and stop his questions. He got that. But…

I still believed her when she said there was no one else.

Anger, this time directed at Julianna, began to simmer within him.

Faith cocked her head as she studied him. "Come down to the station and see for yourself."

Shit. She wasn't going to give him anything else, at least not right then. The sound of Julianna's footsteps reached him, a fast clatter. She hurried toward the detective. "I-I need to call Sophie," she said quickly.

Sophie Sarantos — her defense attorney.

He caught her hand. Pulled her close. To Faith, it probably looked as if he were embracing Julianna, but he wasn't making that mistake. "Yeah, you'd fucking better, baby." Because two dead lovers wasn't good. "And don't ever lie to me again."

Her breath caught and she pulled back, just enough to look into his eyes. "I didn't."

He shook his head. Her breathing was too fast. Her gaze sliding away from his. And her voice trembled. All dead giveaways for deceit. "Bullshit." But they'd deal with her lies...they'd deal with the mess of this case...as soon as he figured out just who the dead man was.

CHAPTER THREE

"I don't know him." Julianna stared down at the pictures before her. Terrible, sickening pictures of a dead man—a man who'd been stabbed repeatedly. Nausea rolled in her stomach because that man—*he'd died just like Jeremy.* The photos showed the dead man sprawled on a brown carpet, a carpet that had a big, red splotch on it. A pool of his blood.

"I'm not in the mood for games," Faith said, her voice hard. No, the detective had never struck Julianna as the playful sort.

Sophie Sarantos leaned across the table and her fingers closed around the picture. Julianna cast a quick glance at her lawyer. Sophie's face showed no change of expression at all, as if looking at a dead man were totally common place for her. "You heard my client," Sophie said. "She doesn't know this man."

Julianna was too conscious of Devlin standing in the far corner of the interrogation room, watching her. She wanted to look back at him, but she forced her attention to stay on the detective.

"If that's the way she wants to play this…" Faith opened a manila envelope and pulled out a photograph. Actually, quite a few photographs. Then she tossed those photographs across the table so that they slid toward Julianna. "You sure look mighty comfortable with a man you don't know," Faith said. "Do you sleep with strangers often?"

It was hard for Julianna to breathe. Way too hard. Because she was staring at photos of herself. Her very naked self. Only she wasn't alone. The dead man was with her. *Not dead. Alive in those pictures. Touching me. Kissing me.* She shoved the photos away. "Those aren't real."

"Oh?" Faith picked up a photograph. Her brows rose as she studied it. "They certainly look real. I mean, this *is* you, isn't it? Unless you have a twin I don't know about."

Desperate, Julianna focused on her lawyer. "I don't know that man. If I slept with him, I'd remember it—"

"But you don't remember killing your husband," Faith said, pouncing on that, "even though you were found with his body and the murder weapon."

This couldn't be happening. Just when she thought things couldn't get worse…

"When was he killed?" Sophie asked.

No, no, that wasn't the question that should be asked. Julianna's hands slammed down on the table. "Who is he?"

Silence.

Then…footsteps, walking closer. Devlin stood at the edge of the table. He picked up one of the photographs. Her hand flew out and grabbed his wrist. "I didn't sleep with him." She'd know if she had. *Just as I should know if I killed my husband.*

No, no, she *hadn't* killed Jeremy. Even if…even if she'd thought about doing it.

But Faith wasn't looking at her. She was focused on Sophie. "Your client *had* psychological evaluations, right? There's no reason for her not to remember—"

"I didn't sleep with him!" She jumped to her feet. Devlin still had that picture of her. He was staring at it so hard and tears were stinging her eyes. She'd thought she was long past tears. "I don't know that man!"

Sophie rose, too, and she put a comforting hand on Julianna's shoulder. "Is there a reason you aren't telling us his identity, Detective?"

"Interesting…" Faith was still sitting. "When we found the dead man, he was lying in a pool of his blood, and all of these pictures of him and Julianna were tossed across the floor."

"That screams set-up to me," Sophie said instantly. "My client is—"

"These are fake," Devlin announced.

Julianna's gaze shot to him.

"Excuse me?" Faith demanded, reaching for the photo.

But Devlin slapped that photo down on the table…and he put it right next to the police shot of the dead body. "Look at the necks."

The what?

"In this picture…" He tapped on the bloody picture. "His neck looks at least two inches shorter." Then he tapped on the picture of the guy — *the guy having sex with me.* "His neck is longer here. Probably because someone pasted his head on another man's body."

And Julianna looked at the picture again. Really looked at it. She was *mostly* naked but…she still had on underwear. A scrap of blue lace. Lace she remembered.

"Look at the wine glass near the bed," Devlin instructed.

Now she did.

"See that curve there? That curve shouldn't be there. The glass shouldn't appear warped like that, not unless someone was playing around with a digital image. Changing things up."

Her gaze slid from the glass to the bed in that image.

I know that bed. "It's the wrong man." Her voice emerged as a husky rasp. "But that's me." In her way too exposed glory. "And that's…that should have been Jeremy." Their wedding night. That wild trip to Vegas. They'd stayed in the honeymoon suite. She remembered that massive bed and the wine glasses…

"It probably *was* Jeremy," Devlin said. "Until someone started playing around with editing tools and that someone spliced this guy's head on Jeremy's body."

But…but those photos meant someone had taken pictures of her and Jeremy together. During their honeymoon. Dammit. *He was always watching. Always.* She'd had no idea just what Jeremy had planned for her. Not until it was too late.

"The dead man's name is Ray Holliwell," Faith said, squinting now as she eyed all of the pictures. "He was a security consultant for Jeremy Smith."

"A security consultant?" Julianna repeated. Her temples were throbbing.

"Yes, we think Jeremy hired him when he wanted to dig up dirt on his competition."

Julianna exhaled as another piece of the puzzle clicked into place for her. *And that's how Jeremy learned my secrets.* He'd paid for some guy to dig up her past and discover secrets that he'd used to control her. To keep her with him when she wanted nothing more than to leave the bastard.

And she *had* been his prisoner.

Until that last night. When she'd had enough. But she couldn't tell the detective those secrets. She couldn't even tell Sophie.

"When did this Ray die?" Sophie asked.

"Yesterday, around 6 a.m., according to our ME." Faith focused on Julianna. "Do you have an alibi for that time?"

Julianna didn't speak.

"Maybe…" Faith's gaze slid to Devlin. "You were in bed with another lover? A living one who can back up your alibi?"

If only. "I—"

"Yes," Devlin said firmly. "Julianna was with me."

She turned toward him, stunned. "Devlin…" She couldn't let him do this.

He stared straight into her eyes and said once more, "Julianna was with me."

She shook her head. Julianna's lips parted—

"I want to speak with you outside, Detective," Sophie said sharply, then she pretty much grabbed the detective and rushed for the door.

Faith frowned, but she didn't fight the lawyer. The door shut behind them, and Julianna asked, voice broken, "What are you doing?"

He leaned in close and put his mouth right at her ear. "Saving your ass." His lips brushed over the curve of her ear and Julianna shivered. "After all, that's what you hired me to do."

But she hadn't hired him to lie. She rose onto her toes. He was still leaning toward her so their bodies pushed together. And it was her turn to whisper into his ear, "But what if I'm guilty?"

***

Sophie Sarantos made sure she shut the interrogation room door firmly behind her. She was really having one hell of a week—near death episodes could be real bitches—and she just wanted to get out of that police station and go climb into the nearest bed with her lover, Lex Jensen. Lex was currently pacing just a few feet away and based on the hard stare he shot her way, he wasn't a very happy camper.

Because we were having one hell of a time...until Faith hauled my client off to jail. "She's being set up," Sophie announced. Wasn't that obvious?

"Oh, I've never heard that one," Faith said, giving a faint eye roll. "No criminal is *ever* set up for a crime that he or she didn't commit."

Sophie just waited.

Faith sighed. "Okay, the pictures do make it look as if—"

"As if someone is out to get my client? The photos were left there deliberately. Let me guess..." Sophie put her hands on her hips. "It was a grand death scene, right? The guy probably had a big envelope or a manila folder right next to his body and it looked as if the photos fell out when he was attacked."

Faith stared back at her.

"Wouldn't she have stopped to—I don't know—pick *up* the photos if they had been legit?"

Faith thrust back her shoulders. "You know I have to follow the trail of evidence. The captain said for me to bring her in…so I did."

Ah, so that meant Faith hadn't been buying the scene, either. But her hands had been tied. "Get your tech guys to look at the photos. They'll back up Devlin." And she would make a mental note that the guy could spot forged photos very quickly. Probably because of his computer skills. Hmmm…if he could spot forgeries so easily, Sophie was willing to bet he could make forgeries just as fast. Another point to file away for future reference.

"Why is he alibiing her?" Faith asked.

I have no idea. "I'll assume it's because they were in bed together at 6 a.m." She made sure to deliberately phrase her reply. *Assume* was such a handy word choice. "Now, the next time you want to talk to my client…" Sophie gave Faith a hard smile. She respected the woman, but she wasn't about to let Faith or any police officer harass her client. "Call me first."

Faith gave a slow nod then she said, "It's not a bad thing that she has protection now."

Oh, hell. She knows that Dev isn't Julianna's lover. Faith knows he's been hired to guard her.

"Because," Faith continued thoughtfully, "if Julianna really is innocent, then it certainly seems she has one very dangerous enemy out there."

Yes, it did seem that way.

Another cop appeared, calling Faith's name. "Excuse me," she murmured as she hurried away.

And then Lex closed in on Sophie. "What the hell is going on?" Lex asked, keeping his voice low.

Ah, where to start? "Your partner has just alibied my client."

He frowned at her. "What?"

"According to Dev, he and Julianna are lovers..."

***

He felt the soft touch of her lips against his ear and arousal shot straight through Devlin's body. He wasn't supposed to get turned on in a police station. There was no way he should be *that* far gone...but his cock was pushing against the fly of his jeans, and Devlin knew he had one serious fucking problem.

He was hot for a would-be killer.

But what if I'm guilty? Her question hung between them. *What if...*

His instincts screamed at him, telling him to protect Julianna.

But he wasn't a fool. He wouldn't let desire lead him down a dark path with a killer. He'd find out the truth about Julianna. He'd discover every secret she'd ever kept. If she was a murderer, then he'd turn her over to the cops, wrapped up in a big, red ribbon.

And if she was innocent, then he'd nail the bastard who was playing such a vicious game with her life.

The best way to uncover the truth? Stay as close as possible to Julianna.

"Let's get out of here," he told her, leaving that *what if* question unanswered. He knew they had to be very careful what they said — and how loudly they said their words. In a police station, eyes and ears were everywhere. He wrapped his arm around Julianna's shoulders and steered her toward the door. When they headed into that hallway, he saw Sophie standing a few feet away, and his friend Lex was at her side.

Lex inclined his head to Devlin even as Sophie hurried toward Julianna. "You're clear to leave," Sophie told Julianna, but there was worry in her blue gaze. "They don't have any evidence to charge you on this one. But…" She cast a quick glance toward Lex, then looked back at Julianna. "I don't like this setup. The car bombing, the murder of the security consultant. Someone is *after* you. Someone with a serious grudge."

Just who would want to destroy Julianna's life? Devlin would be finding out. "I'll be staying close," Devlin assured Sophie. "You don't have to worry. She's under VJS protection now."

"They're the best," Sophie said. Lex put his hand on her shoulder. His gaze met Devlin's. Devlin could easily read the questions in the other man's eyes , but those were questions that would have to wait until later. Right then, his priority was getting Julianna out of there. He took her hand, threaded his fingers with hers, and they walked through the station. Since it was so late, the bullpen was mostly empty. A good thing because he didn't feel like dealing with the suspicious stares of other cops right then.

Once outside, they hurried down the steps and he put her into his SUV. Minutes later, they were cutting through DC, moving quickly in the night.

"Thank you," Julianna said.

He didn't want her gratitude.

I want her. What the hell was it about her? How was she piercing right through his control? His reaction to her was dangerous, mostly because it was so damn primal.

"If you hadn't spotted the problem with those photos, I-I would have been there all night."

He grunted. "Sophie wouldn't let that happen." And the kick in his gut also told him that Faith had probably already suspected those photos were fakes—she'd just wanted to see Julianna's reaction to them. He knew the technique was a cop favorite. Bring a suspect in during the middle of the night—a perfect time when the suspect would be groggy and off-guard. Then, proceed to grill the hell out of that suspect. Toss your evidence at her. Throw out your suspicions.

And watch the person break apart.

Only Julianna hadn't broken apart.

"I...I hate that you saw the photos, though."

They stopped at a red light. A fast glance showed him that she was twisting her hands together.

"It's silly, isn't it? With everything else that's going on, I'm embarrassed because you saw me naked."

Mostly naked. "You don't need to be embarrassed." She had a beautiful body. He'd looked at those images and he'd felt two things.

Desire—hot and hard for her.

Fury—at the asshole in the picture with her. At the bastard who'd taken the picture. At any man who'd touched her.

Because I should be with her.

Yeah, his reactions to her were totally off the charts, and he had to get his self-control back,

pronto. He didn't know what it was about
Julianna that set him off, but he had to be very
careful with her.

The light changed. He accelerated.

"I didn't lie to you."

Devlin could feel her stare on him.

"I didn't have a lover. And I...I hadn't been
with my husband, not since our wedding night. I
couldn't stand the thought of him touching me.
He could make me stay in that house with him,
but I wasn't going to have sex with him. Not after
I-I learned what he was really like."

He nearly slammed on the brakes. He did
tighten his hold on the steering wheel. His grip
was so hard he was amazed he hadn't ripped the
thing right away from the dash. "You weren't
fucking your husband?"

"We were married for two months before he
died. Two of the most hellish months of my life.
We had sex in the beginning of our relationship,
but..." Her voice trailed away. "You were right
about my wrist." From the corner of his eye,
Devlin saw her flex her wrist. "But that was only
the start."

The sonofabitch. He forced his back teeth to
unclench. "He can't hurt you anymore."

Her mocking laughter filled the SUV. "He
can't, but someone else out there sure seems
determined to destroy me."

Yes, someone sure as hell did.

"He was having an affair with his assistant, okay?" Now her voice was even colder. "And I was glad because it meant that he would leave me the hell alone. I might have been stuck in that house with him, but he wasn't going to be in my bed. That wasn't happening." She drew in a shaking breath. "And is there any more of my soul that I have to bare to you right now?"

"Not now," he told her, his voice soft. *But soon, you'll tell me everything.*

***

It wasn't surprising that Julianna had found a new lover. A dumb fool who'd lie for her. She'd probably batted her lashes, fed the idiot some lame-ass story about her past, and the guy had fallen for her.

She would use him, just as she used the others. Julianna was rotten, straight to her core. Others might be fooled by her—

But not me.

The SUV was a few blocks ahead. Julianna was in that vehicle—with the new lover. The lover who'd been there when Julianna's car exploded earlier. *You should have burned, too, Julianna.* Everything had been planned out so nicely. Julianna and Holliwell both should be dead. Two more loose ends eliminated.

Only Julianna was still very much alive and breathing. The police had found the photos of her and Holliwell, and they'd done *nothing*.

At the very least, Julianna should have been thrown into a jail cell. Instead, she was riding off into the night. She wasn't going to escape, though. There would be no happy ending for her.

Soon enough, she'd be joining Jeremy in the ground.

Soon enough…

CHAPTER FOUR

"Okay, buddy…" Lex Jensen paced in Devlin's kitchen. A new day had dawned and streaks of sunlight spilled through the floor-to-ceiling windows. "Want to tell me why you're alibiing that woman? And, hey, do me a favor…save us both some time. Cut through the bullshit and give me the truth."

Devlin took a slow sip of his coffee. He wasn't particularly surprised by Lex's early morning visit. He'd figured that Sophie would tell her lover all about that little chat in the interrogation room. Honestly, he was just surprised Lex hadn't shown up sooner.

"You're a suspicious SOB," Lex continued, frowning a bit. "Hell, you even warned me off Sophie, and we both know what a dick move that was."

Devlin's brows shot up. "I was looking after you. You didn't know if you could trust that woman—"

Lex snapped his fingers together. "Exactly. But you know what I didn't do? I didn't give her some half-assed alibi when she was suspected of murder!" His lips thinned. "You don't usually go lust blind where a woman's concerned. What the hell is so special about Julianna?"

And then he heard it. The faintest rustle of clothing. *Finally*, Julianna hadn't managed to catch him completely off-guard. He shifted position, glancing around Lex, and he saw Julianna in the hallway.

He knew she must have heard Lex's question because her cheeks were flushed. It was rather interesting to meet a woman who could still blush, and he certainly wouldn't have pegged Julianna as that type.

"Um, hi," Julianna said rather awkwardly.

Devlin threw a shark's smile toward Lex. "With all the drama last night, I don't know if you *officially* met our new client. This is Julianna."

Lex swung toward her.

"And this is Lex Jensen."

Julianna was dressed in jeans and a shirt. He'd pulled some strings and his doorman had managed to pick up those clothes from some shop and have them delivered first thing. She looked damn good in those jeans—they hugged her body oh-so-well. Her blonde hair slid over her shoulders as she moved forward to offer her hand to Lex.

Lex's fingers closed around hers. "You don't look like a killer."

Shit. The guy had zero tact.

Lex freed her hand. "But then again, anyone *can* be a killer. It's all about the circumstances, right? About the things that can push us over the edge."

She put her hands behind her back and glanced at Devlin. "Your friend is a serious ray of sunshine first thing in the morning."

Devlin laughed. He just couldn't help it. Her words were the last thing he'd expected.

Julianna's lips curled in the faintest of responses.

Lex didn't laugh. If anything, the guy just appeared grimmer.

"I'm going back to the scene of the murder today," Devlin said, trying to draw Lex's focus. "I want to make sure I fully understand just what went down."

Lex's brows climbed. "There is no way the cops will let you anywhere near Ray Holliwell's place. You know the crime scene techs are going to still be there."

For a while, yes, they would be. But that wasn't the scene he'd meant. "Julianna's house. *That's* where I'm heading."

She wasn't blushing then. She seemed to get a bit paler.

He stared straight at her as he said, "I want to see where Jeremy died. I want you to walk me through every moment that you remember."

She shifted a bit, moving back with her right foot. "Why? You think you're going to magically see something that the cops overlooked?" Julianna gave a negative shake of her head. "It's not going to happen."

"I want to see where he died," Devlin said again. But, more than that, he planned to search that whole house, from top to bottom. Her case was fucked up, and he had to get a handle on it, and her, fast. "Someone tried to kill you yesterday," he said.

"Like I need that reminder."

He wouldn't let his lips twitch. "Don't you want to know why you're in a killer's sights? Because I'm vaguely curious."

"Hell," Lex muttered.

"Vaguely?" Julianna said at the same time.

"We're going to your house." He nodded decisively. "You'll show me where the bastard — I mean, Jeremy — died, and then you'll give me full access to every computer in the house."

"The police confiscated those. Nothing you can use is there now."

He wasn't so sure about that. "I want to see the house, Julianna. I want to see everything."

She nodded. "Okay."

"And while we're checking out that scene…" Devlin glanced over at Lex. "Are you up to learning more about Holliwell?" Lex had been injured — too badly — while protecting Sophie recently. The guy should probably be at home, curled in bed with the delectable Sophie, and not out hunting killers.

"Hell, yeah, I'm up for it," Lex said instantly, but then he stalked toward Devlin. Lowering his voice, he said, "You once warned me not to fall for a client."

Advice that Lex had totally ignored. The guy had been addicted to Sophie from the first moment.

"Maybe you need that warning, too, bro. Just because a woman looks innocent, it doesn't mean that she is." He backed away and inclined his head toward Julianna. "I'll be seeing you both again soon. And, don't worry, I know how to let myself out."

His footsteps faded away. Julianna stood, a bit uncertainly, a few feet from Devlin. "Your friend doesn't like me," she finally said.

He shook his head. Devlin drained his coffee and put down the cup. "No," he said quietly, "he just doesn't trust you. There's a huge difference between the two things."

"I'm not so sure there is."

"Don't worry about Lex. Sophie and I can keep him on track." Sophie wouldn't let the guy go after her client.

Julianna nodded. She turned to leave the room, then hesitated. "Thanks for letting me stay

here last night. I appreciate your kindness, and
I—"

He hurried forward and caught her arm.
They needed to clear up a few things. "I'm not a
kind man." He certainly hadn't ever been accused
of that before.

She looked up at him. Unfortunately, she
looked even sexier to him that day than she had
before—with her hair loose, she was achingly
beautiful.

No wonder Lex was warning me to be careful.
Lex would be able to read him too well, and his
partner would know Devlin wanted Julianna.

Too many men probably wanted her. Did she
use that desire against them? Maybe. But she
wouldn't be twisting him. He could handle
desire. He could fuck her all night long. And
then, if she turned out to be a killer, he could still
walk away.

No problem.

Lex had let his emotions rule him. He'd fallen
fast and he'd fallen hard. Devlin wouldn't be
making that mistake.

"What kind of man are you?" Julianna asked
him, her head tilted just a bit as if she were trying
to figure him out.

He smiled at her and his fingers rose to slide
over the curve of her cheek. "I'm the kind you
don't want as an enemy." *So don't lie to me, baby.
Don't use me…or I'll make you pay.*

***

A prison had never been so beautiful. Julianna stared up at the mansion — a freaking huge historical home surrounded by perfectly groomed acres that stretched and stretched. Jeremy had believed in showing his wealth. Flaunting it. When he saw something he wanted, he took it.

Whether it was a family home that had been protected for generations…like the estate he'd practically stolen from its previous owners.

Or a business that he'd decided he should own, despite the protests of the men and women who'd grown the place from the ground up.

Or…*or me.*

Some days, Julianna hated herself for being so blind. So trusting. She should have learned her lesson long ago. She hadn't.

"So, are we going to hang out here all morning?" Devlin drawled.

Julianna realized she'd been staring up at the mansion for far too long. Flinching a bit, she hurried up to the door. Once, Jeremy had kept a full staff there — maids, a cook, even an honest-to-goodness butler. But he'd gotten rid of most of the staff after her first accident.

Accident, my ass.

She'd given a severance package to the last of the employees after Jeremy's death. She just hadn't wanted anyone there, watching her. No, worse, she hadn't trusted them. They'd been Jeremy's employees. Employees who'd seen what he did to her, and who'd said nothing.

She unlocked the door and stepped inside. As always, the cavernous place felt cold to her. Icy. Rather like a tomb. She crossed the marble floor of the foyer, heading toward the large staircase — a spiral staircase that curved toward the second floor.

Devlin gave a low whistle as he glanced around. "Nice place. I can see why you wouldn't want to leave."

His words pissed her off. There he went — making judgments about her. *And the guy lived in a penthouse!* Like he could really throw stones her way.

Julianna sucked in a deep breath. Then another. She wanted to tell him that she'd been *forced* to stay. But Julianna knew she had to play things carefully. Her life was — still literally — on the line.

Devlin approached her, and in that too big house, his steps seemed to echo. "You been staying here alone?"

"I've been staying at a hotel. I just come back when I need fresh clothes." How to explain that she hated this place? That she couldn't wait to sell it? But selling wasn't allowed, not just yet. Jeremy's will was being held up and Sophie had told her she had to play it cool and *not* do anything that would make her look guilty.

Or, rather, guiltier.

"Show me where you found him."

Right. That's why they were there. Julianna straightened her shoulders and headed into the den. She pointed to the right. "The giant blood stain is gone." Thank goodness. "I had the carpeting replaced in here once the police were done, but Jeremy was there. He died *there*."

"Was he face up or face down?"

She blinked. Julianna had figured he'd read all the gory details already, but perhaps he just wanted to hear her tell him about that terrible night. "He was on his stomach, but his face was turned—turned toward me. His hand was out." As if he'd been reaching for her. She cleared her throat and pointed a bit to the left. "I was here. I mean, I woke up here."

He paced closer to the spot she'd indicated. A positon just a few feet from Jeremy's elaborate bar. Made of old, antique cherry wood, the bar gleamed. Jeremy had always kept that bar well stocked. And the crystal glasses that were oh-so-perfectly arranged on the bar—and on the shelves behind it—shined.

"He was dead when I woke up," Julianna said. She'd told others that same line so many times.

But Devlin didn't reply. Instead, he started opening the bar's cabinet doors.

She frowned. The bar wasn't so well stocked now. "There's nothing here…no booze at all." She cleared her throat. "The cops confiscated everything. I haven't exactly been interested in restocking."

Devlin nodded. "Did you have a lot to drink the night your husband died?"

Again, it was a question the police had asked her, too. "I-I remember having one glass of wine." A glass for courage. That was how she'd remembered it.

Devlin tilted his head as he studied her. "Just one?"

Tell him. If he was going to protect her, if he was going to face the danger surrounding her, then she had to tell him a little more. Not everything, of course, but more of the truth. "That night, I was telling Jeremy that I was done. That I wouldn't stay. That he couldn't make me stay." Her shoulders lifted in a faint shrug. "He gave me the drink, trying to get me to calm down."

"And…did you calm down?"

She rubbed her temples, wishing for the hundredth time that she could remember. "I have no idea. I remember he grabbed my shoulder…" Her hand fell to her shoulder. It had been bruised the next day, bruised with the perfect impression of fingertips. The cops had said that bruise proved she'd fought with her husband — and then killed him. "I don't know what happened after that."

Devlin just nodded.

"Do you believe me?" As soon as she said those words, Julianna wished that she could pull them back. Why did it matter if he believed her? No one else — except Sophie — did. Everybody else in town thought of her as a cold-blooded killer.

"Why were you leaving him then?" He started to pace the room. Opening drawers. Rifling through the books on the shelves. "Why that night, Julianna? What was so special about *that* night?"

I was leaving because I knew he couldn't trap me anymore. Her lips thinned. She had to tread very carefully now. The wrong word would incriminate her and —

"He had an office here, right? Show it to me."

She spun on her heel. "It's not going to do any good." His footsteps followed her from the room. "The cops took his computers. I told you that. There's nothing here for you to find."

"Let me be the judge of that."

They entered Jeremy's study. His desk — a big, antique desk that had cost a ridiculous amount of money — sat in the center of the room.

Jeremy had loved his antiques — he loved anything that he thought showed his wealth and power.

She didn't fully enter that room. She could *feel* Jeremy there. She could feel that bastard everywhere. A ghost that wouldn't stop haunting her.

Devlin began opening the desk drawers. His dark head bent over the desk and for a moment — just a moment — she could see Jeremy. His hair had been dark, too. Maybe a shade lighter than Devlin's. Shorter. Jeremy had been in that office, sitting at that desk. So cold and arrogant as he told her...

I own you now, Julianna. You're mine, body and soul. And if you leave me, I will destroy you.

He'd had the means to carry out his threat. He'd had —

"Julianna?"

She blinked.

"What's wrong?"

She rubbed her arms. "This is a waste of time. There's nothing here to — "

He held up a flash drive. "I found this taped under the top desk drawer. The cops really should have been more thorough when they searched."

Her jaw dropped. Julianna took a quick step forward, then stopped, catching herself.

"Usually, when someone hides a flash drive like this…it's because they don't want that drive being seen by just anybody."

She couldn't take her eyes off that drive. *It was right there, the whole time!* She hurried toward him and reached for it.

But Devlin's fingers closed over the drive, making a tight fist. "Do you know what's on the drive?"

"No." Yes. "How could I possibly?" *It has to be my drive. It has to be!*

Devlin sighed. "You know, I really hate it when you lie to me." He put the flash drive in his pocket. "I'll be checking this on my own. Don't worry. I'll be sure to let you know what I discover."

No! "It's my house. I should have that drive." She lunged for him—very ungracefully—and tried to get her hands on that drive. But he caught her, too easily—and pushed her back. He didn't let her go. His hands stayed locked around her arms.

"My, my…" Devlin murmured, his breath blowing lightly against her. "Someone wants that very badly."

You have no idea. "Give me the flash drive," Julianna gritted out as she straightened.

His eyes had narrowed as they swept over her face. "What's on the drive?"

"It's not a video of me killing my husband, if that's what you're implying." Her laughter was bitter. "The place is uber wired for security, but the system wasn't on that night."

His hold tightened on her. "There are cameras *inside* the house?"

She'd distracted him from the flash drive — good. She would be relieving him of that prize very soon. "Yes. I told you, Jeremy was always watching. Me. His house. Everything he owned." A furrow appeared between Devlin's brows and she mentally cursed herself for that slip. "He had extra security features installed at the house." *So he could watch me and make sure I didn't leave.* "But the system wasn't turned on that night. I checked. The cops checked. Nothing was recorded the night he died." Of course, she knew the cops just suspected that she'd destroyed any recordings, but she hadn't.

They would have proven my innocence.
Right?

"Oh, Julianna…" He said her name almost as if it were a caress. She shivered. "Why are you hiding secrets from me? I want to help you, but you're making it so difficult."

Her heart was racing in her chest. "Please," Julianna said, aware that she was nearly begging. "Just give me that flash drive." *It had been right there, all along. Dammit!*

"Give me the truth," Devlin ordered.

She couldn't, *wouldn't* give it to him. It wasn't just her life hanging in the balance.

"Baby," his voice roughened. "I'm going to look at whatever the hell is on that drive. You can't hide from me forever."

No, no, she couldn't. There was nowhere to hide. There was—

Julianna didn't pull away from him. She pressed closer. She put her body right against his and her hands rose to wrap around the back of his neck. Rising onto her toes, Julianna put her mouth to his.

It was a wild, reckless move. A desperate act to stop his questions.

It was…

What she wanted.

Because Julianna knew that once Devlin learned the full truth, he wouldn't want to be close to her. He wouldn't want to kiss her and touch her and caress her. He wouldn't want to help her.

He'd turn from her, and she'd be on her own.

But I have him now. I can seize this moment — right now.

He was tense, his muscles locked, as he growled against her lips, "What are you doing?"

Screwing everything up. She'd thought that when she kissed him, he'd react—he'd let the desire he felt pour out, wild and hot. Julianna had rather hoped they'd be clawing each other's clothes off in that moment and that all of his questions would be forgotten.

That wasn't happening. Heat stained her cheeks as she eased back enough to admit, "I want you."

"You want the flash drive."

She shook her head. "That wasn't—" *No, I wanted you, before you learned the truth about me from the flash drive.* "Forget it." Could her humiliation get any worse? Probably not. She turned from him and headed for the door.

"You can't leave." Flat. Hard.

For an instant, past and present merged. Jeremy had told her those words, too, right in that same room. Right before he'd shown her the files on his computer. Files that the cops had never found—because they hadn't recovered the flash drive.

Something broke inside of her. Anger and fear and too much pain. "I can do any damn thing I want." She ran, rushing out of the room. Julianna was sick of that place, sick of the memories, sick of the way her life had gone to hell.

He called her name.

She didn't stop. She rushed past the staircase. She lunged for the door.

He caught her. Devlin spun her around and pinned her against the front door. His breath was coming in hard pants and she knew he'd run after her. She hit out at him, desperate right then. Driven too far. "Let me go!"

"Julianna!" He caught her arms and pushed them back against the door, chaining them in place. "What the hell is going on?"

"You don't want me, just let me—"

He kissed her. Kissed her with a wild desire and a molten need. He kissed her the way she'd wanted him to kiss her back in that study.

And Julianna let go. No more holding back, not for her. No more not taking what she wanted.

He was what she wanted. She was going to have him. Right then. Right there.

Screw everything else. If she was going to be locked up for the rest of her life, she'd make sure that she took one incredible memory with her.

CHAPTER FIVE

He should pull back. Devlin knew he should let her go. They should both just calm the fuck down.

But he knew he wasn't letting go. Julianna was rubbing her body against his, kissing him, sliding her sexy little tongue over his lips and into his mouth and driving him beyond all control.

His cock shoved against the front of his jeans. He was so aroused Devlin was sure the zipper impression would line his dick. He wanted in her, right then.

He didn't care where they were. Only Julianna mattered. He'd take her right there.

Right the fuck there.

He freed her hands, but just so he could reach for her t-shirt. He yanked it over her head, tossing it onto that fancy marble. Her white bra — looked like some kind of satin or something — pushed her full breasts up toward him. Hell, yes. He touched her breasts. He shoved that bra out of his way. He lifted Julianna up against him and he put his mouth on her breast, sucking her nipple and loving her taste. Lust pounded through him, heating his veins. He couldn't remember ever wanting another woman this much. Couldn't remember tasting a woman — and feeling lust burn away every other thought.

Her legs wrapped around his hips and she arched against him, moaning low in her throat. That sound just electrified him all the more.

In her. Need in her now. Want her.

He carried her to the stairs. Could he get her up to the top? To her bedroom? Nothing had ever seemed farther away and —

"Now, Devlin," she said, her eyes dark with desire. "*Now.*"

Like he was going to argue with that. Maybe on round number two, he'd have finesse. He'd seduce her. He'd taste every inch of her body and he'd make her scream. But right then, if he didn't get inside of her, Devlin was sure he'd go insane.

He lowered her, but only for a moment. Only long enough for her to kick away her shoes and for him to drag down the jeans that covered her hips. And when her jeans went down, so did her panties.

He almost forgot to breathe. She was so fucking perfect. Flaring hips. A bare sex. Built for temptation. Built for *him.*

"No one else is here," Julianna said. "I want you…don't make me wait anymore." Her voice was husky and far too seductive. He wasn't making her wait for anything. He pushed her back, lowering her on the stairs. Every inch of her body was silken temptation. She reached for him, but he caught her hands.

"Baby, I'm holding on by a thread."

She licked her lips, a quick swipe of her pink tongue. Sexy as hell. He bent over her. His hands slid along the silken expanse of her thighs and he parted her legs, opening her fully to him. His breath sawed from his lungs as he stared down at her. He wanted to drive deep and hard into her, but he needed Julianna to be ready for him.

Because he sure wasn't planning a nice, easy fuck.

Hard. Deep. Wild.

He put his mouth on her sex. Her hips heaved up against him, but Julianna didn't push him away. Her hands flew over his shoulders and her nails sank through the fabric of his shirt. She urged him closer and her legs slipped open even more.

He licked her. Stroked that perfect pink flesh. Savored her taste, got drunk on it. His fingers slid over her, and she was wet now — from his mouth, from her own arousal. She gasped out his name and rocked her hips against him. Asking for more. Demanding her pleasure.

Pleasure he couldn't wait to give to them both.

His fingers slid inside of her. She was warm and tight and she was going to feel fabulous. But he had to make sure there was no pain for her. Had to make sure that she was right on that edge of sanity with him.

His fingers pushed into her, moving faster now, a little rougher, even as his mouth found the center of her need. He worked her clit with his tongue and loved the way she trembled beneath him. Trembled and—

"Devlin!"

Came.

He surged up. Devlin yanked a condom out of his wallet and had the thing on in about two seconds. He shoved his jeans down, and then he was driving into her. No hesitation. No restraint. He thrust into her as deep as he could go.

Their eyes met. He could see the pleasure on her face. The wildness in her gaze that came from the fury of a climax. He locked his arms around her hips and hoisted her closer. Her sex closed eagerly around him, so tight he was going insane. He withdrew, thrust deep, and heard her sweet moan again.

Would she come for him one more time? He sure hoped so.

Again and again, he thrust. He had her pinned to the stairs. He kissed her, wanted to damn near devour her. Pleasure hummed along his nerve endings, but it wasn't enough.

Need in deeper. Want more. Want everything.

He couldn't hold back. He should have. He should have kept some control, but the fury of desire rode him hard. Her legs were around his hips, her body fitting his so perfectly, and when he felt the contractions of her sex around him — *coming again* — Devlin erupted. His release blasted through his whole body, a pleasure so intense that he could only growl her name. He was too lost, too fucking gone — too fucking caught up in the best damn climax of his life.

On the stairs.

With his jeans around his ankles.

In the house where her husband had been murdered.

That is fucked-up.

His eyes squeezed shut as he fought the urge to keep thrusting. To take her again, endlessly. To go wild with her and let the rest of the world just fade away. Because in that moment, he could truly almost think that nothing else — and no one else — mattered. Just her.

Just the pleasure they could give to each other.

But he felt her legs slowly slide away from his hips. Her breath was coming in little pants and when he heaved up to look down at her, she looked…

Beautiful.

But there was hesitation in her eyes. Maybe even fear? Shit, no, he didn't want her afraid of him. Not Julianna.

Then maybe you shouldn't have fucked her like a lunatic on the stairs.

He should apologize. He should get his cock out of her and not think about what a hot heaven she felt like. He should do a thousand different things right then.

He kept staring into her eyes.

She pushed up toward him. Her hand reached out and slid over the stubble on his cheek. Then she kissed him. Not a passionate, hot kiss. But…soft, almost sweet, in the aftermath of the maelstrom that had consumed them both.

His eyes closed and he just wanted to savor her. Instead, he very slowly pulled away. Her hand slid down his arm, over his jeans, then back to her side.

He righted his clothes quickly, jerking his jeans back up and zipping way too fast. Then, with care—care he hadn't been able to show her before—he pulled Julianna up to her feet. His hand caressed her shoulder because he was having a really hard time *not* touching her. "I'll get your clothes." From wherever the hell he'd thrown them.

Part of Devlin was horrified by what he'd just done. Fucked her there—taken her *there*, so close to her husband's murder scene. How screwed up did he have to be? And another part—the dark, twisted part—just wanted to have her again.

He found her bra, dangling from the bannister. A quick search turned up her shirt. He gave those back to her, then took her jeans and the scrap of her panties to her. Sexy panties that he really hadn't appreciated in the heat of the moment. She dressed quickly, in silence, and that silence tore at his gut. If ever a woman needed care—shit, why hadn't he been able to slow down a bit?

"I'm sorry," he said. Devlin didn't apologize often, but she deserved his remorse. She deserved flowers and chocolate and him swearing not to be a bastard any—

"Don't be." She was fully dressed now, even her shoes were back on. But her cheeks were flushed and her eyes gleamed. "I'm not sorry. I wanted you. *Here.*" She gestured around the house. "The ghost doesn't own me, and it was far past time for me to take my life back."

His brows climbed at that. "So you're—"

The lock jiggled behind them. He whirled at that tell-tale sound about two seconds before someone unlocked the door. He lunged forward, wondering who would have a key to Julianna's place, even as that door swung toward him.

A woman with long, blonde hair stood in the doorway. She wore a sleek suit and her green eyes — a deep, dark green — narrowed on him. "Who the hell are you?"

"I was about to ask you the same damn question."

Her eyes brightened with fury *and* alarm. "I'm calling the cops! Get out of Jeremy's home!"

"Avery?" Julianna said. Then she pushed past Devlin. "What are you doing here?" She shook her head. "And how *dare* you just let yourself into my home?"

If the woman had let herself in a few minutes sooner, she would have gotten quite the show.

Avery's disdainful glance swept from Julianna to Devlin, then back again. "It's not your home," Avery said, ice dripping from her words. "It's Jeremy's. You don't belong here. You need to just drag your sorry ass out…but I guess the cops will be doing that soon enough."

He didn't like Avery. Not one bit. He stepped forward.

But Julianna put her hand on his chest. Avery's cutting glance noticed that move. "Did you *seriously* bring your new lover into Jeremy's home?" Avery took an aggressive step forward. "You slut, how dare you—"

"Yes, he is my lover," Julianna said that without even a hint of embarrassment.

He blinked at her calm words. Now he wondered…if Avery had arrived a few minutes earlier, would Julianna have cared? *I don't think so.*

"You might think your boss was a saint, Avery, but I've got a news flash for you," Julianna said. "Jeremy was a twisted, sadistic bastard. He was only happy when he made others miserable. "

Avery sucked in a shuddering breath. "You can't talk about him like that."

"I just did." Then, in an impressively fast move, Julianna reached out and yanked the keys out of Avery's hand. "Don't ever come into this house unannounced again. You do, and the police will be hauling *you* away. Not me."

Avery's cheeks paled. "I just needed to check his desk. I-I'm working on a deal that needs to be closed and I thought he had the files at home."

"Then you should have called me to get them. Not broken into my home." Julianna's voice dripped ice.

There was plenty of fury in Avery's stare. Fury and hate.

"Go search for the files," Julianna ordered curtly. "Then get out."

Avery shoved past her. Her shoulder hit Julianna, and Julianna grunted at the impact.

He caught Julianna's hand in his. "What the hell is happening? Who is she and why did you let her inside?" Didn't Julianna realize the other woman hated her with a killing fury?

Julianna sighed. "Avery Glenn is — *was* — Jeremy's personal assistant."

With *personal* being a keyword there. That woman was way too attached to her dead boss.

"The company is still running. It employs hundreds of people, and the board is in charge. I mean, I own a majority share now, but they're running things. If I weren't under investigation for Jeremy's murder…." Bitterness entered her voice. "I'd just sell all my shares back to the board and get out of this mess. But I'm stuck, for the time being." Her gaze swept around the house. "Stuck in this house. A grave above ground."

Avery came stomping back. He'd never seen a woman stomp in high heels, not until then. "The files aren't here," she announced. Her glare said the missing files were Julianna's fault.

Julianna shrugged. "Then there's no need for you to be here, either."

Avery stalked up to her. But then her gaze cut to Devlin. "She seduced him, too. Seduced him, used him, then killed him. Right here…in the same place she probably fucked you."

Julianna tensed.

"Do yourself a favor," Avery said, shaking her head. "Run, don't walk, away from this woman. If you don't, she'll wreck you, too."

Julianna grabbed the door and held it open for the other woman. "Ah...even better than a greeting card. Avery, your charm never wanes."

Avery actually growled. Interesting.

"Get the hell out," Julianna said. "Come back and the cops will greet you."

Avery marched out. Julianna slammed the door shut after her. Devlin noticed that Julianna's hands were shaking. So she wasn't as in control as she'd want him—or rather, Avery—to think. "I can't stand that woman," Julianna said softly.

I think the feeling is mutual.

Her gaze slid to him. "For the record, I never had sex with Jeremy on the stairs."

"Good to know." He didn't like thinking about her having sex with that bastard—or any other man. *Only me.*

"Not the stairs. Not the bedroom. Not any place here. This house was nothing but a prison for me, and I hate it." Her lips twisted. "Right, and I know that just makes it sound like I had even more reason for killing him, doesn't it? Avery certainly thinks I killed him." Her hands rubbed over her eyes, then dropped to her sides. "I don't even know why he wanted me. They were sleeping together long before we met."

They—Avery and Jeremy?

She sighed. "Are we done here? Please say we're done. I want to leave."

He cleared his throat. "Yeah, we're done here." *For now.*

"Good. I-I need to go to Sophie's office," Julianna said as she hurriedly opened the door. "There are some papers for me to sign there."

He'd drop her off, and then he'd head to VJS and find out just what waited on that flash drive.

Clouds were filling the sky, and it was fucking cold outside. They locked the house, and they headed for his vehicle.

That was when he realized that Avery hadn't left. She was still in her car. Still glaring at him and Julianna. His hand was on Julianna's back as he steered her toward the SUV, and Devlin knew they looked like lovers. He used his remote to unlock the car and to start the engine. After that explosion, he wasn't about to take any chances with *any* car, not any longer.

There was no explosion, a good thing.

"Out of curiosity," he murmured as he opened Julianna's door. "Just where was Avery when your husband was killed?"

"She was working at the office. Alone." She slid into the seat and looked up at him. "The cops already had their killer, so they didn't exactly waste a lot of time on her."

The cops had their killer.

"You said she was the one sleeping with him?"

"Yes." Her voice was stilted.

Interesting. That might explain some of the woman's fury toward Julianna. "He married you, but fucked her."

Julianna drew in a sharp breath.

He slammed the door. "Bet that sure pissed her off."

At that moment, Avery cranked her car. Her tires screeched as she raced away.

***

"It wasn't there," Avery said as she swiped at the tears on her face. "I looked in his office, but I didn't find the file."

"Then you just need to look harder," the male voice said, filling the interior of her car as it drifted through her speakers.

"I can't. Julianna kicked me out." As if that were her home. As if Julianna had any right to be there at all. After the hell Avery had been through, that place should have been *hers*.

"She was there?"

Her foot pressed down on that accelerator, driving faster and faster as fury filled her. "She was there with some guy—it was obvious that I interrupted them." Julianna's mouth had been swollen, her hair mussed. And the guy—

"Who was he?"

"I don't know. Just the dumbass of the moment." A fool who'd probably been lured in by Julianna's delicate facade. Men could be such fools. "Tall, dark-haired, with blue eyes." Eyes that had unnerved her. "Why can't she just be locked up? The cops should have her in a cell!"

"She'll be taken care of, don't worry."

So he kept saying. He hadn't seen Julianna. Hadn't heard her.

"We have to find that file," he told her. "If we don't, Julianna won't be the only one heading to jail. Just keep your focus, Avery. I *need* you."

And she needed him. They were the perfect team. He'd been there for her all along, but he didn't know…

He never realized I was with Jeremy. He didn't need to know that. Sex with Jeremy had been wild, hot, and more than a little dangerous. She'd liked his danger.

"Tell me I can count on you."

Her foot eased off the accelerator. "You can count on me. For anything."

***

Julianna stopped at the entrance to Sophie's law firm. She turned and smiled up at Devlin. "I've got it from here," she told him softly. "Thanks."

He brushed back her hair. His knuckles grazed her cheek. She shouldn't have felt his touch like an electric charge that shot through her body, but she did. She was far too attuned to him.

I want him far too much.

When he'd apologized back at the house, she'd desperately wanted to stop him. The last thing she felt was remorse for what they'd done. She'd wanted him, he'd wanted her, and she hadn't been about to let her past control her anymore. She was out of that prison now.

"I'll send Chance over to keep an eye on you," Devlin said and she knew he was talking about Chance Valentine, the other partner at VJS. "I'll go back to VJS and review the flash drive—"

"Chance doesn't need to come." She'd never officially met Chance, but she knew his reputation. The guy was one top-notch security expert. She didn't need him to be anywhere close to her right then. "I'll be here with Sophie for at least the next hour. Maybe two. When I'm done, I'll call you."

A faint furrow appeared between his brows.

"I'm perfectly safe here. There's plenty of security. Really, I'm fine. Go take care of that drive."

He nodded, but he didn't look happy.

"Devlin—"

His hand slid down to curve under her chin. "Dev."

She blinked at him.

"My friends call me Dev."

Is that what they were now? Friends? She'd rather thought they were lovers. "Mine call me Julie." The few that she had.

His thumb brushed over her mouth, a sensual slide across her too-sensitive lower lip. Then he leaned forward and kissed her. This kiss was far different than any they'd shared before. The desperation was gone. The wildness was tamed.

But...

It was sensual. Maybe the most sensual kiss she'd ever had. His lips stroked over hers, seemed to savor her. The kiss was open-mouthed, but he took his time, first sliding his tongue lightly over her lower lip, then dipping it inside her mouth.

Her hands rose and pressed to his chest as she arched up even higher on her tip-toes. It had been too long since she'd wanted a man with abandon. Too long since she'd been swept away. Too long since—

Jeremy.

A chill skated down her spine.

Devlin—Dev—slowly pulled back. He stared down at her, his gaze unreadable, then he said, "I want you again."

She nodded. "I want you, too." Truth. Maybe it was dangerous, but the desire was there. Far stronger than it should be.

"Tonight, I'll have you again."

Promises, promises.

He took off his coat and wrapped it around her. "The snow's starting to fall," he said a bit gruffly. "Go on inside."

She hadn't noticed the snow. She hadn't really noticed anything but him. She caught the edges of his coat and pulled it closer. Then she turned and headed into the law office. The glass doors shut behind her even as Matt, the guy who pulled double-duty as a receptionist at the law firm and as a body builder—rose in greeting.

"Ms. Smith?" Matt called. "What are you doing here?" He glanced down at his desk. "I don't have you on the calendar."

She peered over her shoulder and watched Devlin drive away. Her hand slid into the pocket of her jeans and curled around the flash drive, a drive she'd slipped away from Devlin without him even noticing. "I'm so confused," she murmured and grimaced. "All the stress…I think it's getting to me."

He nodded sympathetically.

"Will you do me a favor?" Julianna asked. "Call me a cab? Please?"

"Of course." Matt instantly reached for his phone.

Good. Because I've got someplace I have to be.

CHAPTER SIX

Devlin stopped at the red light. His fingers drummed on the steering wheel. He didn't like leaving Julianna alone. His body was tight with tension, worry. Something was off. Just…wrong.

His hand slid into his pocket, looking for the flash drive. Maybe that little drive could help Julianna's case.

Only…that little drive wasn't in his pocket.

He had a sudden flash of Julianna. She'd been sliding her hand down his arm. She'd brushed her fingers over his hip.

And that woman took the flash drive right out of my pocket!

What the hell? Just where had Julianna Patrice McNall-Smith learned to be a pick pocket?

A car horn honked behind him. Swearing, he accelerated because the light had changed — who knew how long ago — but he quickly pulled a U-turn and rushed back to Sophie's law firm. When he was a few blocks away, he saw the unmistakable flash of Julianna's blonde hair.

She still had his coat on and she was waiting at the corner of the street.

So much for a meeting with Sophie.

Hell, didn't the woman get it? He was trying to help her.

But she was…what? Lying to him? Stealing from him?

Seducing him? Avery's accusation flashed through his mind, but Devlin shook his head. Fuck, no, he'd been seducing Julianna just as hard. That hadn't been any kind of one-way street. Yet the knot in his stomach told him this whole set-up was wrong. Innocent people weren't supposed to lie. They sure as shit weren't supposed to trick the bodyguard that had been hired for protection.

A taxi pulled up at the curb. Julianna instantly jumped in the back of it, and the cab took off. Devlin waited for two cars to get between him and that taxi. He waited, then he began his pursuit. Julianna wasn't slipping away from him. This wasn't amateur hour for him, despite what she might think. She wasn't going to manipulate him.

He was there to protect her, but he was also there to find the truth. With every second that passed, the suspicion within him grew ever stronger. *Innocent people don't lie. They don't run.*

He knew that with certainty. His parents hadn't been innocent, not by a long shot. They'd run. Far and fast. And they'd left him behind.

Just as they'd left a wake of destruction in their paths.

Had he been wrong to let down his guard with Julianna? Hell, he'd been blindsided by her from the beginning. He rarely ever looked at a person and saw a victim, but from the very first moment, he'd looked at Julianna and just wanted to protect her from everyone and everything that might hurt her.

He kept following that cab. Maybe she was just going to a hotel. Or perhaps even going back to VJS Protection or —

The cab stopped. It didn't stop in front of a hotel and that building sure wasn't VJS. The car had braked in front of a club. One that was, unfortunately, too familiar to Devlin.

Wicked.

It was a club owned by a fellow that Devlin couldn't stand on the best of days and on the worst of days — well, he figured Ethan Barclay was a straight-up killer. VJS had been through enough run-ins with the guy that Devlin knew the fellow was trouble.

Why was Julianna going to his place?

Devlin braked near an alley. For just a moment, he remembered another night. A night that he'd gone running down that exact alley. At the time, he'd thought that Ethan had been stalking his buddy Chance's lover, Gwen Hawthorne. Devlin's job had been to go around back, to seal off that escape route.

Too late, Devlin had found a killer waiting back there for him. *Not* Ethan Barclay, but a man who'd made it his mission to destroy the club owner. Devlin had been caught in the crossfire, and he still had the battle wounds to prove it. He'd been left in that alley, bleeding out, with the garbage, and he'd been sure that he was dying.

Julianna exited the cab and ran toward Wicked.

Why is she going to him? Devlin had been digging into Julianna's life. He'd found *no* connections to Ethan Barclay.

But maybe he hadn't dug deep enough.

The door to Wicked opened and Julianna disappeared inside.

Devlin turned off his vehicle. He stared at the club and he knew that twist in his gut—it was suspicion.

It was also jealousy.

Why is she going to him?

***

"You weren't supposed to come here, Julianna," Ethan said as he headed toward the bar. The club was empty, and Julianna knew

Wicked would stay that way, until dark. When the sun set, Wicked always came alive. "The plan," he continued, as he downed a gulp of what she thought might be whiskey — she'd never been too savvy on her drinks, "was for you to stay safely away from me. You already look guilty enough without me dragging you down into the mud anymore."

Her heart stuttered a bit at those words. Most folks thought Ethan was the bad guy. And, well, truthfully, he wasn't a *good* guy. But he wasn't evil, either. She stared at him a moment, her gaze sweeping over his face. Once, he'd been the perfect embodiment, the tall, dark, and handsome ideal. But that had been before a twisted bastard named Daniel Duvato had attacked Ethan with a knife. Now, twin scars marred Ethan's perfect cheeks. He was still handsome, but definitely with a dangerous edge.

"No one can look away," Ethan muttered as his fingers rose and brushed over the scar on his left cheek. "At least now I look like a villain."

"Stop it," she told him. "Play that game with someone else. Someone who doesn't know you. Not me." She pulled out the flash drive and put it on the bar. "I had to come over because I found this." She hesitated. "Actually, Devlin found it. The drive was taped under one of Jeremy's desk drawers."

His hand closed around the flash drive.
"Devlin?"

"Devlin Shade. He's a body guard," Julianna
rushed to explain. "He works for—"

"VJS." Ethan appeared pained. "Sophie
referred you, right?"

She nodded. "You know him?"

"Unfortunately, I know him and his
buddies." He shook his head. "And I'll tell you
now, he isn't going to be happy about this little
visit."

"He doesn't know I'm here. I-I took the drive
and ditched him."

Ethan's lips quirked. "Old habits die hard,
huh, Jules?"

Jules. Ethan was the only one who'd ever
called her that. She'd been telling the truth when
she told Devlin that her friends called her Julie.
They did. Ethan didn't qualify as a friend. Not
exactly.

He lifted up the flash drive. "Let's see if this
is the one."

Her heart beat faster. "How will we know if
he made copies? I mean, what if—"

The cry of an alarm broke through the
interior of Wicked. She jumped at the sound.

"Easy." Ethan didn't look at all ruffled.
"After that knife-wielding asshole came in here
and tried to carve me up, I instituted a few new
security measures." He turned away and a few

seconds later, a screen appeared behind the club's bar. The shelves of glasses slid back, revealing a flat screen. He tapped on his phone, and an image appeared on that screen.

"You didn't ditch him," Ethan said flatly.

Devlin's furious features filled the screen.

Oh, crap.

Ethan glanced at her. "How is this going to play out? I can tell you now, he's not just going to walk away. He'll stay there until he gets in, and then, the way I see it, we have two options."

She couldn't look away from Devlin. He definitely looked pissed. Julianna swallowed.

"Option one. We tell him the truth. Unfortunately, I think the guy is one of those freaking Boy Scouts. You know, the kind that really gets on my last nerve. With his history, he could have gone either way."

His history? She finally managed to glance back at Ethan.

"But Devlin decided to put the bad guys away." He quirked a brow. "He might think you're one of the bad guys."

Was she? "I-I…" Dammit, why couldn't she remember what had happened the night Jeremy died?

"Option two." He shoved the flash drive into his pocket. "We lie our asses off. You don't owe that guy anything, Jules. I'll back up any story you want to give him."

He would. He'd backed her up before.

"So what's it going to be?" Ethan asked her.

Julianna squared her shoulders. "I had sex with him."

Ethan swore. "Because you just *wanted* to make things more complicated?"

Her gaze strayed to the screen—and to Devlin's face—once more. "No," she told Ethan quietly. "Because I just wanted him." But he wouldn't see it that way. Not if he realized she'd taken the flash drive. He'd just think that she had been trying to distract him. That she'd used him.

She hadn't.

She'd been free with Devlin. She'd been able to let herself go and just feel. The house that had been a prison for so long—she'd broken out, with Devlin. No pain. No fear.

Only him.

Devlin lifted his hand and pounded on the door.

"Let's turn on the audio," Ethan murmured. He tapped his phone again and sound came out around her as—

"Open the fucking door," Devlin snarled. "I know she's in there. Now…Let. Me. In."

***

Someone had gone slumming.

Julianna Patrice McNall-Smith had certainly shown her true colors. From a mansion to the darkest club in the city. It had just taken a few clicks to get pictures of her rushing inside Wicked so desperately. Going to see Ethan Barclay?

Maybe he was still her weakness.

But now the new lover had joined the fray. From the looks of things, he was about to tear down the door in order to get to Julianna. A jealous lover could be a very dangerous thing for Julianna. A jealous lover could be pushed to the edge…so very easily.

Time to learn about that lover. Time to see how he could be used.

Then eliminated.

***

Devlin lifted his hand. Ethan needed to hurry up and open that damn door. His fisted hand swung toward the wood once more—

The door opened. Julianna stood before him, and his hand hung in the air, far too close to her beautiful face.

"I—" Shit. He dropped his hand.

Julianna backed up a step. Had fear flickered in her eyes? He didn't want Julianna afraid of him. Never that. He'd like to kick the crap out of Ethan, but he would *never* do anything to Julianna.

"You should come inside," Julianna said. She swung the door open a few more inches and Devlin saw Ethan, standing far too close to Julianna. "I'll explain everything inside."

He crossed the threshold and marched right up to Ethan. "Why is it…" Devlin gritted out. "That every time I turn around, I'm tripping over you?"

Ethan smiled. A cold, dangerous smile.

Devlin just glared right back at him.

Julianna shut the door. "I had enough violence with Jeremy. Don't even think of swinging a punch right now." Her gaze cut between them. "That goes for both of you."

And Ethan's face softened. "I'm sorry. If that bastard were still alive—"

"Ethan…" A warning edge entered Julianna's voice.

But Devlin knew what the guy had been about to say. Maybe because he felt the same way. *If that bastard were still alive, I'd kill him.*

Julianna's left hand curled—rather protectively—around her right wrist.

Ethan locked the door. "Come this way. We should go into my office."

They didn't speak again until their little group was inside Ethan's office. A place that was filled with fancy leather furniture. Devlin's sweeping gaze took note of the giant screen that took up a whole wall. He saw that a desk was near the far right of the room, and a computer waited on top of it.

"Let's just save some time," Devlin said as he crossed his arms his chest and inclined his head toward the computer. "Put the flash drive in and show me the contents, *now*."

Ethan glanced over at Julianna.

"I know she took it." Did he look like a moron? "What I don't know is why she ran straight to you."

Ethan shook his head. "Oh, Devlin, I'm afraid you have this all wrong—"

"No." Julianna's voice was sharp. "He doesn't. He has it all right." She moved to stand in front of Devlin. "I took the flash drive from you."

She sounded…miserable. Guilty.

"But don't even think…" Now her finger jabbed into his chest. "Don't think that me having sex with you had anything to do with the flash drive."

"Oh, shit," Ethan muttered.

Devlin caught her hand. "How the hell am I supposed to think anything else?" She'd wanted the drive. He'd had it. She'd—

"I wanted you. I still want you. That house was hell for me. Being with you there, I was breaking free. Of Jeremy. Of his cage. I was *living*. You gave me so much pleasure…" Her breath shuddered out. "What we did had nothing to do with the flash drive, I swear it."

He stared at her. Devlin wanted to believe her but… "You never had a meeting with Sophie."

She shook her head. She didn't try to pull her hand from his. "I had to meet Ethan."

Why did it just feel as if someone had shoved a knife into his heart? Not someone—her. "Who is he to you?"

"Someone I owe."

"That answer isn't going to cut it, baby. I want the full truth from you, and I want it now."

Ethan sat down behind his desk. His leather chair squeaked. "Why do people always run around demanding the truth? They don't really want it. *You* don't want it, Devlin. You want to go around, living in your happy bubble and pretending that bad things don't happen."

Bullshit. He squeezed Julianna's hand, then stepped around her, directing his attention on Ethan. He didn't let her go, though. He wasn't sure if he could.

So how fucked up am I?

"I know bad things happen," Devlin snapped.

Ethan looked him up and down. "Because your parents were some of those…bad things?"

Devlin fired a quick glance at Julianna.

"What?" Ethan drawled. "You want all her dark secrets, but you don't want to share your own? I can dig into a person's past, too, you know. And yours was so easy to obtain. I mean, when two people go on a spree like your folks did, it does tend to make the news. They killed — was it four? Five people? — before the cops took them out. They were on drugs, right, and — "

"They were high for most of my life." He couldn't look at Julianna right then. Not when he talked about this part of his life. "I don't remember them any other way. They were young and they were wild and they didn't care about anyone but each other." He sure hadn't thought they ever cared about him. But his grandmother had. She'd taken care of him. Tried to protect him.

Until his parents had died. Gone out in their blaze of glory. And the people from DHR had come to take him away from his grandmother. Suddenly, they'd decided she was the unfit one.

"You swore not to be like them, right?" Ethan's fingers tapped on his desk. "Your buddies Chance and Lex — they went off to be true blue soldiers, but you were different. You stayed here. You got a job with the FBI."

Julianna's hand jerked in his grasp and she tried to pull away. He didn't let her go.

"You're with the FBI?" Her voice came out as a high squeak. "You — you can't be!"

He shrugged. Julianna was definitely worried now, not a good sign. "I was." He put a deliberate emphasis on *was*. "I have a knack with computers. I learned early on that I could use that knack on the wrong side of the law." A side that his parents had been too familiar with during their lives. "Or I could try to make up for some of the pain my family caused." And he had. He'd worked with the cyber unit for years, unraveling so many secrets. Learning that the polite world he saw truly was just a thin veneer of deception. Real monsters were out there, and they were everywhere.

When Chance had come to him with the idea of opening VJS, he'd agreed. Devlin wasn't sure if Chance even realized the truth about all the work he'd done for the FBI. Sometimes, Devlin didn't even want to think of the cases.

Because he hadn't just stayed with the cyber unit. He'd gone out on missions, slipped into the darkness…

And wondered if I'd ever get back into the light.

Julianna was still trying to pull free. He was still keeping his hold on her. He was afraid if he let her go right then, he just might lose her. He glanced toward her.

"The FBI," she said, shaking her head. "I am so screwed."

He frowned at her words.

"How much of her past…" Ethan said, drawing Devlin's attention, "have you already discovered?"

"Apparently, not enough," Devlin fired back. "Because I didn't realize she was involved with you." That fact pissed him off. Just how involved had they been? Friends, lovers? And when?

Ethan Barclay was trouble, and Devlin hated for Julianna to be any place near the guy.

Ethan's fingers drummed on the desk top once more. "I know lots of people. You'd be surprised at the folks who owe me favors in this town."

"She's your friend," Devlin said.

Ethan inclined his head. "So it would seem."

"Then explain to me…" Now fury pumped through him. "Why you let your *friend* stay with that bastard? He broke her wrist. He hit her—"

Julianna gasped. "Stop—"

"I saw the hospital records," Devlin nearly snarled. "Sophie is building your defense, remember? It was easy enough to access those files." Child's play. "He didn't just hurt you once. He hurt you over and—"

"I tried to leave a second time, all right? I tried!" Her voice was too sharp.

Ethan shot to his feet. "Julianna…"

Her shoulders straightened with pride. A pride that made Devlin's chest ache. "He thought he controlled me when he hurt me. He was wrong. I was just biding my time with him."

Ethan paled. "This shit never should have happened! I would have taken care of him! I would have—"

"The flash drive," Julianna whispered. "I had to get it, no matter what."

For an instant, a red haze swam in front of Devlin's vision. "You were abused because you were protecting this bastard?" First Sophie had tried to protect Ethan, and now Julianna? What. The. Fuck?

"No." Julianna's voice was sad. "It wasn't for him."

Silence.

Ethan's gaze was on Julianna.

"Who?" Devlin demanded. Who had she endured that pain for? Who the hell was it?

Julianna cast a worried glance his way. "You don't have to turn over evidence you find today, do you? I mean, if you're not FBI any more, maybe you can just let the past go."

That ache in his chest got worse. "What are you covering up?" His fingers slid along the inside of her wrist, a caress that he couldn't help even as he waited to see just how much trouble she was really in.

Julianna swallowed. "I'm covering up a murder."

CHAPTER SEVEN

"Uh, Jules," Ethan said, his voice more than a bit strained. "If Sophie happened to be here right now, this is the part where she'd advise you to stop talking."

Devlin had turned to face her. There was no expression on his face. A very big part of her wondered if she were making a terrible mistake. She'd certainly made her share of those over the years. Perhaps she was making another one right then. But lying to Devlin just didn't seem right.

When she'd been with him earlier, she'd felt a connection that had been real. True. He'd seemed to actually *see* her—the person she was, and not just the woman she spent so much time pretending to be.

"My sister." As soon as she said those words, Julianna knew there would be no going back now. "I'm protecting her." That was her job, wasn't it? As the older sister, she was supposed to protect Carly, no matter what. She'd screwed up before, but she'd been determined to help her sister this time around.

But Devlin shook his head. "I didn't turn up a report of any sister in your background check."

"She's not my blood sister. My mother's second husband…" Oh, but her mother had enjoyed her marriages—all of them. "He had a daughter. Carly. My mom only stayed married to him for a few months before she moved on." She'd moved on to much greener pastures because Carly's father had been too much of a dreamer, and not a "doer" for her. "But I kept in touch with Carly. She was family."

Ethan nodded. "You should understand that, Devlin. Didn't you and your VJS buddies form your own family in foster care?"

Devlin had been in foster care? Julianna's eyes widened. She didn't—

"Carly murdered someone," Devlin said, his words sharp.

"Sh-she was protecting herself," Julianna tried to explain. "She was…money was tight, okay? I wish she had told me sooner, but Carly was trying to support herself and her dad. She was only seventeen and she was—"

Ethan stood up. "I found out she had gotten a job dancing at a club. One she had *no* business being in. Julianna and I found out at the same time."

Julianna glanced toward Ethan. He always tried so hard to keep his voice expressionless when he talked about Carly. He was good at wearing his mask, too.

"The owner of that club became obsessed with Carly. I got her to quit," Julianna said and she hated that painful memory of Carly. Her humiliation. Her tears. "But he kept coming after her. Saying that she belonged to him. He was following her everywhere."

Ethan strode from around his desk. "I told the bastard to back off, but those days, I was just some twenty-one year old punk to him. He didn't fear me."

Not like today. Julianna knew too many people feared him today.

"He came after me," Ethan said flatly. "He and his goons had me pinned down and they were beating the hell out of me." His hand lifted and he held the flash drive out to Devlin. "You can see the rest for yourself."

Ethan's fingers finally released their hold on Julianna's wrist.

She said, "One of…one of Quincy's men made the video." Quincy Atkins. Would the name mean anything to him? The D.C. crime boss who'd vanished years before. "I didn't even know it existed, I mean…why the hell didn't the guy come forward sooner? I had no idea about it, not until I tried to leave Jeremy." Her back teeth clenched together. "He had it. He knew."

Devlin headed toward Ethan's computer. He inserted the flash drive and tapped on the keyboard. A few mouse clicks later, the video opened. Julianna crept forward so she could see the screen.

A much younger Ethan was on the dirty floor, bleeding. His face was smashed to hell and back.

Carly was there, her long, dark hair streaming down her shoulders. She was tied to a chair, screaming, begging for Quincy to stop hurting Ethan.

Quincy waved his hand and his men rushed from the room.

Then Quincy — a big, hulking jerk of a man — took the knife from the sheath at his hip. "I'm gonna cut Loverboy open," Quincy boasted. "Then you'll be mine. Body and soul. I'll own every inch of you…and *no one* will ever be able to help you again."

Tears poured down Carly's face. "Please," she begged in that video. "Don't hurt him anymore. Don't. I'll do anything — just *don't!*"

But Quincy lunged toward Ethan. He kicked Ethan in the ribs. Again and again. Then he rolled Ethan onto his back, holding the knife right over Ethan's heart.

In the present, Ethan cleared his throat. "Too many bastards are always coming at me with a knife," Ethan said then, his shuttered gaze on the video. "Why the hell is that?"

Julianna's stare slid back to the screen. She saw Carly tear free of the ropes that bound her. She saw her sister lunge out of the chair. "*Don't hurt him!*"

Carly slammed into Quincy. They flew over Ethan's body and the knife…

Carly rose. The knife was in Quincy's chest. The handle stuck out, but the hilt was in him. Quincy opened his mouth, as if to call out to the guards.

Carly put her hand over his mouth. Tears streamed from her eyes. Her body shuddered.

Ethan crawled toward her. A trail of blood was left in his path. His hand lifted…

And he shoved that knife even deeper into Quincy's chest.

The video stopped.

Nausea swirled in Julianna's stomach. "Jeremy showed me the video. H-he told me that he'd make sure Carly went to prison. That he'd destroy her." She pushed back her hair, aware of the quiver in her fingertips. "Quincy raped my sister. He terrorized her. After that…after his death…she broke down. It took so long for her to get her strength back. But she finally moved past that night. Put it totally behind her. She has a new life now. She's thriving in New York. She…she's safe." Julianna swiped at the tear that had slid down her left cheek. "I just wanted to keep her that way."

Devlin took the flash drive out of the computer and put it in his pocket.

And it was right then that Julianna realized...she was still wearing his coat. His warmth had been surrounding her the whole time.

But now he knows.

She shrugged out of the coat and put it across Ethan's desk.

"How did Jeremy Smith get the video?" Devlin's voice sounded far too calm to her ears.

She and Ethan shared a quick glance.

"No lies," Devlin warned. "Just the truth."

"That night," Ethan said quietly, "I was interested in getting Carly out of that place. I...I called a friend to help with clean up." He smiled bitterly. "You might know that friend — Daniel Duvato." He rubbed at the scar on his right cheek. "He's the bastard who went psycho and tried to kill me. It seemed he'd been keeping that little video, waiting for the perfect moment to burn me with it. When Jeremy's security guy came sniffing around a while back, Daniel gave it to him...for a price."

"Let me guess." A muscle flexed in Devlin's jaw. "Was that security guy named Ray Holliwell?"

Ethan nodded. "That would be the bastard."

*Oh, Dear God...*Julianna hadn't realized — the man who'd been murdered had been so mixed up in all the madness. She tried to think, to plan, to look for a way out of this mess. "Ethan wasn't the only one who'd get burned if that video is given to the cops," Julianna said, trying to make Devlin understand. "Carly would, too. I wasn't there for her before. I didn't help her. I wasn't going to make the same mistake again."

Devlin swore. "You know what this is, right?"

She held her breath, waiting.

"This is fucking motive, Julianna. It's the perfect motive for you to kill. Not because that sick bastard was hurting you — not that defense anymore. Shit, this is motive because you wanted to stop him from exposing your sister. It's a motive for you to kill him *and* Ray Holliwell."

She knew what it looked like. "What are you going to do?" Because that was what mattered. Would he turn the flash drive over to the police?

"I don't fucking know." He marched around the desk. He grabbed the coat and put it around her shoulders again. "For now, we're getting the hell out of here. I have to think."

Ethan stepped in their path. "I know you want to burn me." A muscle flexed in his jaw. "You and VJS all think I'm scum. I get it. You're wrong, but fuck that." He exhaled roughly. "If you turn in that flash drive, you're burning *them.*

Julianna doesn't deserve that. Neither does Carly."

Devlin stepped toe-to-toe with him. "Your enemies stretch for miles, and they just keep coming."

"I'm popular that way."

"You ever stop to think that one of those enemies may be after Julianna? Maybe someone knew her husband had that flash drive, knew that it would implicate *you*, and that person is doing anything necessary to get his hands on the damn thing. Even if that *anything* includes killing Jeremy Smith and putting a bomb in Julianna's car." He shook his head in disgust. "Why do others have a way of getting hurt around you? Gwen, Sophie—"

She saw Ethan's face harden, and she knew that Devlin's words were hitting their mark.

No. "Stop it." Julianna pushed between the two men. And she directed her growing fury at Devlin. For too long, she'd had to guard her emotions. She'd had to walk on freaking egg shells until she thought she'd break with Jeremy. But he was gone and she was *free*. She'd take her life back now. "Ethan's my friend, and you don't talk to him that way."

Surprise flashed on Devlin's face.

"You can be angry. You can be pissed because you think I misled you."

"You *did* mislead me," Devlin muttered.

"But Ethan was trying to help my sister. No one else was there for her. Not even me." That hurt so much to admit. "And Sophie will be the first to tell you…Ethan is a good man." She glanced over her shoulder at him. "Even if he doesn't always think so."

Devlin swore.

Ethan looked away from her. "You should go with the bodyguard, Julianna." Then he pulled her close and pressed a kiss to her brow. "And you stay safe."

She nodded.

He eased away from her and bumped lightly into Devlin. His hand brushed over Devlin's side, a would-be aggressive move. "You keep her alive, or you'll see just how dangerous I can truly be. I'm not some punk kid anymore."

"Save your threats for someone who gives a damn."

"Stop it," Julianna gritted again, driven to the edge. "We have to focus on what matters right now."

Devlin glanced at her. "You're right." He pulled her closer. "You matter."

He…well…

"You matter," Devlin said again.

Then he was guiding her away from Ethan. She didn't look back. She knew exactly what Ethan had done a moment before, and really, it was for the best, wasn't it?

One nightmare over. Only a few dozen more to face.

Devlin took her outside. He led her to his SUV. She couldn't help but tense when she drew closer to it. She wasn't going to be looking at cars the same way for a very long time. The last few times she'd gotten into a vehicle, her stomach had knotted and she'd remembered the lance of fire on her skin.

Devlin stopped her before she'd gotten too close to his SUV, and he lifted his remote, cranking the car with the press of a button. It growled to life—and, wonderfully—didn't explode.

Her relieved breath slid out.

"I know," Devlin said as he brushed the snow off her cheek. "I know what the jerk did back there."

Her head tilted as she stared up at him.

"Is Ethan the one who taught you how to pick pockets?" Devlin asked her.

She pressed her lips together, then admitted, "He and Carly were close when we were younger. When mom and I lived in the area…yes, he taught me." Ethan had always known such interesting things.

"You're better than he is,' Devlin said as his fingers lingered near her cheek. "I didn't even feel it when you took the drive."

His hand started to fall away.

She caught it. Held tight. "His life is on the line, too. He doesn't —"

"Trust me?"

She nodded. The snow fell down onto them. It had started to fall heavily while they were in Wicked.

"What about you?" Devlin shifted ever closer. "You told me the truth. Does that mean that you trust me? How do you feel, Julianna? How do you feel about me?"

"I…" Was she supposed to trust him? So soon? Probably not. Another mistake. She'd thought that she knew Jeremy and she'd been dead wrong on that score. She'd sworn never to be blinded again, but…

Devlin had deserved the truth in Wicked. He was working to protect her.

He…

"You don't trust me, not fully, not yet." He didn't sound angry. In fact, his voice was tender. Warm in the cold. "That's okay, baby. I can wait."

She stared into his eyes, not understanding him at all.

"I can wait as long as you need."

That was nice. Maybe the nicest thing she'd heard in a very long time.

But then his gaze slid away from hers. He frowned as he looked over her shoulder. "Someone's watching us."

Her muscles locked.

"In a blue SUV, sitting at the curb. Tinted windows."

If the windows were tinted, how could he be sure they were being watched?

"The vehicle isn't covered in snow…it's warm. Running. Someone is in it right now."

She spun around, looking for that vehicle. She found it—and saw the tinted window rolling down. Down…

"Gun!" Devlin roared and he locked his arm around her stomach and yanked her to the side, hurtling her down behind his vehicle.

A shot rang out. A blast that thundered and had her gasping. Then she heard the squeal of tires as the shooter raced away.

Devlin's body was on top of hers. The freezing snow was below her. He lunged up, swearing, as he looked after that fleeing vehicle. She sat up, moving much slower. She brushed off the snow that covered her clothing.

"Are you all right?" Devlin asked.

She was on her feet now. His hands slid over her body, checking for injuries. There weren't any. The bullet had hit his vehicle, not them. *Not this time.*

A bomb. A bullet. What would come next?

"Jules!"

Ethan raced toward her. Fear had turned his normally tanned skin ashen.

Devlin moved his body in front of Julianna's, his pose protective.

That was sweet and all…and she'd hired him to protect her but…*I don't want him taking a bullet for me.* She didn't want anyone doing that.

"I saw her on the security feed." Ethan's breath heaved out. "I thought that bullet was going to hit you."

"Her?" Devlin said, voice dangerously soft.

"The shooter. I saw her blonde hair when she lowered the window." His lips thinned. "And I got her tag number, not that we need it. I recognized her."

"Who the hell was it?" Devlin demanded.

Ethan's hands were clenched at his sides. "Heather Aslo, Jeremy Smith's step-daughter." His golden eyes glittered. "The woman who's been so busy telling all the reporters that Julianna is a murderer."

CHAPTER EIGHT

"There's some mistake." Heather Aslo smiled at Detective Faith Chestang. "I haven't shot anyone. That's absolutely crazy!" Then her gaze jumped to Devlin. "And who are you? Are you a cop, too?"

He smiled back at her. "Nice innocent act. But you know exactly who I am. I'm the man you had in your sights less than an hour ago." He had to give the DC cops credit—or, at least, give credit to Faith. She'd moved fast and had taken Heather into custody even before Devlin and Julianna made it to the station.

Julianna was currently waiting in another interrogation room. Because Faith owed him a favor or two, she'd let him come inside for this little chat. He wondered how many lies Heather would tell before they got down to the truth.

Heather's smile dimmed a bit. "I didn't try to shoot you."

Faith nodded. "Right. I know you didn't."

Heather looked relieved.

"I think," Faith continued, seeming to really consider the matter, "that you were aiming for your step-mother, Julianna—"

"She's not my step-mother!"

Oh, wow. Someone had anger issues. That would probably explain the bullet in the side of his ride.

"Officers are searching your home and your vehicle right now." Faith's voice was still as mild as you please. "They'll find the gun, and they'll match it to the bullet that we dug out of Devlin's car."

A furrow appeared between Heather's brows. "Devlin?"

"That would be me," he told her, giving his own slow, cold smile. "Devlin Shade. I'm Julianna's bodyguard, and one of the witnesses to your little shooting attempt."

Heather's gaze slid to the door. "Do I need a lawyer?"

Why, yes, you do.

Faith slid a sealed envelope across the table. One of those big, cushioned envelopes.

"What's that?" Heather wanted to know.

"A security video." Faith was still calm, polite. "One of the nearby businesses had it."

Ethan Barclay had been the one to give the video to Faith.

"That video," Faith continued, "shows *you*, in your vehicle. It shows *you*, firing at Julianna."

A tear slid down Heather's cheek. "She's the killer, not me."

Devlin crossed his arms over his chest. "Julianna wasn't the one shooting the gun."

Heather leapt to her feet. "I wanted to scare her! She's out, walking around town, hanging out with all kinds of men!"

All kinds?

"She killed him, and I wanted her to pay! I wanted her to be afraid! I wanted her to know —"

Heather broke off and slapped a hand over her face.

But Devlin wasn't about to let that go. "Just what did you want Julianna to know?"

Her hand slowly fell. "That she wasn't going to get away with what she'd done."

Faith glanced at him. "I think we've found Julianna's stalker."

"She *killed* him!" Heather yelled. "He took care of me, always took care of me! And when he was going to leave her, she flipped out. She stabbed him. Avery told me! She told me what Julianna was really like. Julianna wants the world to think she's good, but she's a cold-blooded bitch! She —"

Devlin sighed. "She wasn't the one shooting in a public street."

Heather gulped. Her gaze darted to Faith.

"Tell me..." Faith asked. "Just how many times have you wanted to...*scare*...Julianna lately?"

"I-I..."

Faith tilted her head and asked, "When Julianna's car exploded, were you just trying to *scare* her then? Did you want her to know...oh, yes, 'that she wasn't going to get away with what she'd done' to your step-father?"

Heather backed up. But there was no place for her to go. Her shoulders hit the interrogation room wall. "I want a lawyer," she said, her voice whisper-soft. "I'm not saying another word, not without a lawyer."

Faith nodded. She collected her notes and the still-sealed envelope and made her way to the door. When Faith and Devlin exited, a uniformed cop took their place inside with Heather. Faith spared Devlin a hard look. "Having a VJS rep down here is starting to become a trend. Can't you guys find a way to stay out of my station?"

He shrugged. "Maybe if people would stop gunning for our clients..."

Her lips twisted. Not a smile. Not a frown, either. But her eyes gleamed a bit.

"Can I take Julianna out of here?" Devlin wanted to know.

"With her stalker locked up, she should be safe now," Faith said.

She should be. Would that mean that she didn't need a bodyguard any longer? "You're so sure that Heather was the one who set the bomb? I mean, how did she learn how to do something like that?"

"I've been doing some checking…" Now she did smile. "You know, as a detective, that's what I do. It's not like VJS solves all the crimes in the city."

He knew exactly how smart Faith was. Chance had worked with her, years before, at Hawthorne Industries. The woman was sharp, fair, and one hell of a cop.

"Heather's boyfriend has explosives training," Faith said. "Courtesy of Uncle Sam. It doesn't take a big leap to figure that he might have given her some how-to training."

Or to figure that he could have even set the bomb for his girlfriend. Devlin's lips thinned.

"I've already got officers bringing Hugh Bounty in," Faith said quickly, "and, no, you don't get to sit in on that interrogation." Her head inclined toward the interrogation room on the right. Julianna's room. "Take your client out the back. I heard that the reporters are already out front in a feeding frenzy. Maybe you can escape them. Maybe not." Faith turned away.

"Do you think she did it?" Devlin asked.

Faith looked over her shoulder. "The woman just confessed, Dev. She said—"

"Julianna." *Not Heather.* "You were the arresting officer on her case. You know criminals." He stared into her eyes. "Do you think she did it?"

"Oh, please…tell me you aren't falling for that woman."

He shook his head.

"You'd better not be lying," Faith muttered. "Look, *all* of the evidence pointed to her. Julianna was saying she couldn't remember what happened the night before. That she blacked out, but the woman had no history of any blackouts. That shit was just far too convenient."

"He was hurting her."

Faith's lashes flickered. "I never said Jeremy Smith didn't deserve killing. But it's not my place to be someone's executioner."

"You think she did…" Dammit.

"We did blood work. Just checking, you know, to make sure she hadn't been drugged. I mean, hell, maybe she'd been roofied. That would explain the blackout and memory lapse but…"

"But?" Did she really need to trail off like that? The woman was killing him.

"But the tests showed nothing."

The tests didn't always show positive results. Especially when too much time had elapsed. "That doesn't mean she wasn't drugged."

"Rohypnol. GHB. Zolpidem. Temazepam."
Faith's voice roughed with disgust. "These days,
nearly anything can be slipped in a drink."

"So she *might* have—"

"Her prints were on the knife. Blood spatter
was on her." Faith's brows climbed. "So if you're
crawling into bed with that woman, I'm going to
advise you to sleep with one eye open." She
paused. "You should also lock up your knives.
Jeremy Smith was stabbed thirteen times. That
sure tells me his killer had a whole lot of rage
tapped inside of her."

"Heather Aslo has plenty of rage."

Faith seemed to absorb that. "She wasn't
found next to the dead body." Once more, her
head inclined toward interrogation room number
two. "Go get your client and get her out of the
station. I don't particularly enjoy feeding the
reporters when they're in their frenzy." She
sauntered away.

Squaring his shoulders, Devlin headed for
the second interrogation room. A cop wearing a
stiff-looking uniform stood at that door, his body
at strict attention. Devlin knew the guy had been
eavesdropping on his whole conversation with
Faith.

When Devlin approached, the cop quickly
opened the door. Devlin strode inside.

Julianna was seated at the small table. She
was still wearing his coat and still looking far too

fragile in its broad mass. Her head turned and she gazed at him with eyes that had never seemed quite so dark before. "It was her, wasn't it? All along."

"Faith thinks so." He wasn't on board with that idea, not yet. He wanted more evidence first. "Come on. The reporters are outside and we need to get out of here."

She nodded and rose. Her steps were a little slow as she headed toward him. "I can't...talk to her?"

"She's not talking to anyone right now." *Not until her lawyer gets here.* "And, baby, that woman has a whole lot of fury directed at you. The last thing I want is for you to be in a room with her."

They made their way to the back of the station. They were going to have to hurry over a few blocks and get a cab. Maybe the reporters wouldn't see them, if they were lucky.

He wondered who had tipped the reporters off to the new story. Devlin would personally like to thank that asshole.

"Come on." They moved fast as they hurried out of the station. Another cop he knew held the door for them, and they rushed out. He kept a tight grip on Julianna's hand as they sprinted across the streets and away from the reporters. He could see a cab up ahead. They were almost there—

"Mrs. Smith!"

Shit.

"Mrs. Smith," a male reporter demanded as he ran after them, "is it true that your step-daughter tried to kill you?"

Devlin whirled toward the man. "No comment."

The reporter's green eyes narrowed. "I'm not asking you, buddy. I'm asking the lady." The fellow was nearly as tall as Devlin. He peered over Devlin's shoulder, trying to see Julianna. "Did she blow up your car, too?"

"Devlin," Julianna whispered. "The cab is close. Let's go."

He turned with her. But the reporter lunged forward and grabbed Julianna's hand, yanking her back.

"Do you deserve to die?" The reporter blasted. "Is Heather right? You killed, so it's your turn to be killed?"

Devlin grabbed the guy by his shirt-front and shoved him back. The reporter's blond hair was mussed, and flecks of snow drifted over him. "Get the hell back!" Devlin ordered.

"You can't stop me!" The reporter blasted. "I have a right to question her, I have a — "

They climbed in the cab. "Get us out of here," Devlin said.

The cab zoomed away. Other reporters had raced to the curb, but they were too late. Devlin shook his head in disgust. "Is that really the shit you've been dealing with?"

"I think that was John Reynolds," Julianna said as she glanced out the window. "He works for the DC Journal. He was the...the first reporter to demand my arrest."

Figured. "He's an asshole." Devlin hadn't liked the way the guy wrapped his hand around Julianna's wrist. He brought her wrist to his mouth and pressed a quick kiss to her skin.

"Wh-what are you doing?"

Honestly, he had no fucking clue. He was so tangled up over her. *Sleep with one eye open.* He stared into her eyes, and he didn't see a killer. Could she really be that good at deception?

He kissed her wrist again. The wrist that Jeremy had broken. The wrist that jerk had grabbed. "I want you to stay with me tonight."

The cab braked. "Okay, buddy," the driver called back. "I got you away from them, now tell me...where are we heading?"

Julianna held his gaze. Then she nodded.

Devlin rattled off his address to the guy and when the cab turned, taking them back to his place, Devlin interlocked his fingers with hers. He didn't know where this thing with Julianna was going to lead him, but...

I'm not ready to lose her yet.

***

Heather Aslo stared at her reflection in the interrogation room mirror. She knew the mirror was only on her side. On the other side, someone else was watching her. Waiting. Probably cops. No doubt, it was that female detective, Faith Chestang.

Faith thought Heather was trying to kill Julianna.

You're right, Faith. I am.

Because Jeremy had told her…Julianna wasn't the woman she pretended to be. He'd told her that Julianna was dangerous. He'd said that if anything happened to him…

Look to Julianna.

It had been obvious when Jeremy was killed that Julianna was responsible. She'd carved him up. Stabbed him again and again. Heather had been the one to go down to the morgue. She'd seen the mess that Julianna had made of Jeremy's body.

It had almost looked as if she'd tried to cut his heart out.

You won't get away with what you did. She wasn't going to let it happen.

A knock sounded at the door. It opened seconds later, and Heather saw the familiar figure of Harry Gibbs in the doorway. Harry had been Jeremy's lawyer for years, and now, he was hers.

"I-I don't have a lot of criminal defense history," Harry began nervously. "But I can refer you to—"

"Forget the referral. You'll be fine." Because she didn't intend to stay in jail. All she needed was to get public opinion on her side. "I need you to get John Reynolds in here, now. Got it?"

"John Reynolds?" His bushy brows climbed. "The DC Journal reporter?"

She nodded. "You'll find him outside. Get him in here…because I've got a story to tell him."

Harry glanced toward the mirror. "I don't know…"

"Get him in here." She stared in that mirror, too. "If the cops want me to talk to them anymore, then they'll give me time with John. I don't care if they listen to every word we say, but I'm talking to him." *Do you understand me, Detective? I'll talk plenty, but I'm going to make sure the right people hear my story.*

She wasn't going to rot in some jail cell while Julianna was out living it up with her new lover. No way was that going to happen.

John would help her. He always did.

CHAPTER NINE

She should go to bed. She should just walk away from Devlin. Go in the guest room. Shut the door.

Get as far away from temptation as possible.

She *should* do that, so why was she just standing in the middle of Devlin's den, her hands twisting in front of her?

Julianna peered over her shoulder. Devlin had lit a fire and the warmth filled the room even as the flames cast flickering shadows over the walls. Darkness had definitely fallen in the city. She used to love the dark.

Before Jeremy.

Before her life had gone to hell.

"You look like you could use a glass of wine," Devlin said as he headed toward the bar in the corner of the room.

Wine. Yes, that sounded good. She turned toward him—

But for just a moment, his den vanished. Devlin vanished. Instead of the cozy fire, ice seemed to wrap around her. Julianna could have sworn that she was back in Jeremy's home. In *his* den. He was making her a drink.

"*I've told you, Julianna. Divorce isn't an option for us.*"

"*But why? You don't…you don't love me. I don't love you.*"

He laughed and handed her a wine glass. "*What the hell does love have to do with it? You're mine, I want you. And you're staying…mine.*"

She stared down into the wine glass. So red. Like blood.

"*Drink up, sweetness.*"

She hated that endearment. He'd called her 'sweetness' right after he broke her wrist. Right after the time he'd slapped her when they left the big charity party. He'd waited until they were in the limo, then he'd struck…telling her that she'd been flirting…right in front of him.

No one had ever hit her before him. No one had ever hurt her physically. Not until Jeremy. Not until the man who'd vowed to love her and honor her. She'd been stunned at first. Surely it couldn't really be happening?

But it was. It had.

"*Drink your wine.*" *His voice had hardened, taking on the edge that told her his temper was stirring.*

When would he hit her again? She didn't know, but it couldn't go on. She wasn't going to let it. She refused to be his fucking punching bag for the rest of her life. "I'm leaving." *Her fingers curled around the stem of the wine glass.*

"Leave…and your darling little sister will get her ass thrown in jail."

Julianna shook her head. "I won't let you do that."

He drained his glass. "Let's see you try and stop me."

"Julianna?"

She jerked at Devlin's voice and the memory vanished. She was back in Devlin's den. The fire was warming her skin and he stood before her, offering her a glass of…red wine. Her lips felt numb as she said, "I don't drink red wine."

"Oh, sorry." He put down the glass. "I can make you anything you want."

She didn't want to drink anything. She didn't want to eat anything. She didn't want to talk about how twisted and tangled everything was.

She wanted him. "Will you make love with me?"

He stilled.

Okay, right. Love had nothing to do with it. He didn't love her and she didn't know if she could ever love a man again. When you made such a colossal mistake in judgment once, how could you risk that pain again? "That wasn't…" Julianna cleared her throat. "I want you." There. That was good. Basic. Honest. "Do you want me?" Could it be simpler than that?

His hands were loose at his sides. "Baby, do you even need to ask?"

"I'm not looking for promises." They should be clear on this. "I don't want forever. I don't want you to swear that you'll always be mine."

His eyelids flickered.

"I want tonight," she said. "I want you. I want no regrets. I just want as much pleasure as we can handle."

His gaze held hers. "And everything else? Your sister? The charge against you? Your stalker?"

She hated to think about all of that. "My sister is in New York. She's safe. The murder charge against me is going to be taken care of — I've got the best lawyer in the business." A lawyer that Ethan had recommended to her. "As for my stalker, she's locked up." She still couldn't believe it had been Heather. Heather had hated her enough to take a shot at her? "So I don't have to be scared anymore. I can relax and be with you."

He wasn't taking her into his arms and giving her one of those awesome-devastating kisses of his. He was just staring at her, his eyes glittering, and she realized that desire might not be enough. Not for Devlin. "You don't trust me," Julianna whispered.

His head inclined. "You do like your secrets, don't you?"

"I told you the truth."

"*After* you ditched me so that you could run to Ethan." Now he moved toward her, a slow glide that made her tense. "So before we do anything, we need to get a few things straight."

Her breath came a little faster. "Maybe this was a mistake. You don't want me so—"

His hand slid around the curve of her shoulder. "I want you. More than I've ever wanted another woman. I look at you, and I ache. I look at you, and I want to be *in* you."

Okay...

"That's the first thing we need to get straight."

With an effort, she swallowed the lump in her throat. "I want you...so much that it should scare me." Because she hadn't planned to give herself to another lover, not so completely, not with the wild abandon she'd had with him...*in that terrible house.*

"Are you afraid of me?" His voice was rough, but his gaze seemed worried as it swept over her.

She didn't answer, not at first, because it wasn't an easy yes or no question. How did you trust a man when you'd seen how much violence another could deliver? Were you just supposed to put that fear away and act like nothing had ever happened? She couldn't do that. "Yes, I'm afraid."

He stepped back. His hand slid from her.

She lunged forward and grabbed his hand. "I'm afraid of the way I feel about you. I'm afraid that I feel too much, far too soon, with you." And she'd thought that she'd gotten caught up with Jeremy too soon…the attraction she felt for Devlin was *nothing* like what she'd felt for her dead husband. "I'm afraid because…" She would be brutally honest here. "Because we've just met and I'm already in too deep with you. Your past is violent, your job is violent, and I don't want to ever be anyone's victim again." *I won't be.* She'd do whatever was necessary to protect herself.

Even kill.

A muscle jerked in his jaw. "I swear, I will never hurt you."

She wanted to believe him. She'd also wanted to believe that Jeremy couldn't have actually hit her or broken her wrist or —

"I am not him," Devlin said with cold fury, but his fury didn't seem to be directed at her. "I am not like that bastard, and I never will be. I would sooner cut off my own damn hand than ever lift it against you or any woman."

She was holding his hand. A strong hand, tanned. A hand that could form a powerful fist. A hand that had caressed her so carefully.

"I have rules, Julianna. My rules. I never hurt anyone weaker than me. I think the worst kind of bastard in the world…that's a bastard who hurts a woman or a child. A man doesn't do that shit. Not a real man."

Her mouth had gone dry. She swallowed again, quickly.

"You said you're not looking for promises," he added, his voice still holding that gruff edge of anger. "Too bad, baby. Too bad. Because I'm about to give you one."

She shook her head. "Dev…"

"I promise, I will never hurt you. I will *never* raise my hand against you, and if anyone else does…if anyone ever so much as puts a faint bruise on your skin, I will make the sonofabitch pay."

She couldn't look away from the brilliance of his eyes.

He cleared his throat. "Now, I'm not perfect. Ethan was right about me. My parents…they were criminals. Killers. The cops took them out in a blaze of glory — my parents were high on drugs and it took a storm of bullets to stop them. I think I was six at the time."

Her heart ached for him.

"I don't remember them much, and maybe that's a good thing because I *don't* want to be like them. When I bounced around the foster homes, the story about my past would follow me. I'd hear the whispers. I'd hear the social workers saying that I should be 'watched' more because of my past."

The ache in her heart was getting worse.

"Most people thought I was trash. I got that. But then one day, I met my brothers."

Her brows lifted. He had brothers? But—

"Chance Valentine and Lex Jensen. We wound up in the same group home at the right time. They looked at me, and they didn't see the past that hung over me like a dark cloud. They saw me." His shoulders rolled back in a hard shrug. "And I saw them."

Brothers.

"We moved around after that, but the bond stayed. I knew they'd always have my back, just as I had theirs."

So maybe he could understand how desperate she'd been to protect her step-sister. Family wasn't always about blood.

"I'm not perfect," Devlin said again. "But you can count on me, Julianna. I won't lie to you. I won't deceive you. And when you need me, I'll be there for you. No matter what."

Her lips lifted in a smile she couldn't control. "You really are one of the good guys, aren't you?"

"Don't let that get around." He didn't smile back at her. But his hand turned and locked with hers. "So the choice is back to you. Knowing everything now…do you still want to be with me?"

Julianna nodded. "Even more." Did he have any clue just how sexy he was? Sex appeal wasn't always in a man's looks or the hard lines of his body—though Devlin was pretty hot that way. No, sex appeal came from just who the man was…and how he treated a woman.

She pushed up onto her toes as he bent toward her. Julianna's mouth skimmed over his in the lightest of kisses. "There aren't any stairs here," she told him and she nipped his lower lip. "So what are we going to use?"

He laughed softly and Julianna realized that she quite enjoyed that delicious, rough rumble. "I have a king-sized bed we can use."

"That sounds—" Her words ended in a surprised yelp because he'd just picked her up in his arms and he was carrying her down the hallway to his bedroom. He held her easily, as if she didn't weigh anything at all, and she realized just how strong he truly was. For a moment, her heart stuttered and her nails dug into his arms.

He froze. "Julianna?"

The breath she sucked in felt cold.

This is Devlin. Jeremy is gone. He can't hurt me anymore.

She pulled her nails out of his skin. She made herself smile at him.

His lips found hers and he kissed her, using such tender care. "You have my promise," he told her.

This is Devlin.

When he pulled back, her smile was real. He strode down the hallway with her cradled in his arms. They entered the bedroom, and it was dark, so very dark, with only faint moonlight drifting through his blinds. But Devlin didn't seem to have trouble navigating. He moved easily through that room and slowly lowered her onto the bed. She expected him to follow her down. He didn't. Devlin eased back, and she heard the rustle of his clothing.

Julianna pushed up on her elbows. Her eyes strained to see him in the darkness. He was a big, hulking shadow — a shadow that was stripping quickly, judging by the sounds she heard. That was a nice change, considering that he'd pretty much been fully clothed the last time they were together.

His shadowy form stepped toward the bed. She sat up fully then, reaching for him. Her hands touched warm skin — then moved along what sure felt like an incredible six pack. Her mouth followed her hands. Kissing lightly.

He sucked in a sharp breath. "Julie…"

She nipped him.

"Fuck, baby, I am trying to hold on to my control."

She started kissing a path that would take her lower. "Why? Who asked for control? I like it when pleasure makes us both go wild." And she went a bit lower. Her hand touched his cock, a fully erect cock that sprang toward her. Wide and full. She stroked his length, moving from base to head, again and again. He growled and she loved that sound.

Julianna bent forward and put her mouth on him. Her lips closed over the head of his cock and she licked him, sliding her tongue over the sensitive skin before she took him in a little deeper.

His hands curled around her shoulders. He didn't push her back. Didn't shove her forward. He just held her. "You're driving me crazy."

No, not yet, she wasn't. He should give her more time.

She licked again. Sucked. Julianna savored him with her mouth and tongue. He swore but he still didn't move. He was letting her explore him. Letting her have all of the power, and she got a heady surge from that control. The big strong guy, at her command. Shuddering, for her. He was—

"*Enough,*" Devlin growled.

No, she didn't think it was nearly enough. Not for her and not for him. But she found herself tumbling back on the bed as he loomed over her.

His hands went to her feet. There were soft thuds as her shoes hit the floor. She ditched her shirt and shoved down her jeans, but he was there to help, tugging the jeans — and her panties — out of the way.

She still wore her bra. Maybe she should get rid of it. Maybe she should —

"You want to be fair, don't you, baby?" Devlin asked.

Her racing heartbeat seemed to shake her chest.

"I know you do…so I get my taste, too."

He pulled her to the edge of the bed, bent, and put his mouth on her. Her teeth sank into her lower lip because it was either bite that lip or let go and *scream*. What he was doing to her felt so insanely good. He knew just how to touch and lick and stroke and she was about to climax already —

He pulled away. She heard him fumble with a nightstand drawer and then Devlin came back to her. Her hands slid over his back as she yanked him closer. She'd been too near the edge and now she was frantic for him.

But…

He lifted her, holding her easily, and he put her on top of him. Her knees pressed into the bedding on either side of his hips and his cock brushed against the entrance of her sex. She was wet already — both from her arousal and his mouth and when Julianna arched down against him, his cock slid deep into her with one hard, hot glide. She moaned at the sensual sensation, not even trying to hold back her cry.

"You are so fucking sexy," Devlin said.

He made her feel sexy.

They were in the middle of the bed, and his hands were tight around her hips as he lifted her up and down. She moved faster and faster, driven to find her release. Her breath choked out, her heart raced, and she clamped her muscles tightly around him. He was so thick and full within her, and her climax was coming, she could feel it drawing closer and closer.

Her hands flew out and curved around the headboard. Using that grip, she moved harder, took him in deeper with the wild thrust of her hips.

"*Yes,*" Devlin said. "Hell, yes." And his right hand rose to shove her bra out of the way. His fingers stroked over her nipples, tugging, and a bolt of sensation seemed to shoot straight from her nipples to her sex.

She pushed down on him, rose up, drove down again. She needed to come. She was so close, that release tempting her —

His upper body reared up and his mouth closed around one breast. He sucked her nipple, a strong, hard pull, even as his hips surged against her again. She went over the edge, and Julianna cried out. She yelled her pleasure, she shook…she felt like she damn well quaked as that release rolled through her whole body.

"Fucking sexy…" Devlin's voice roughened even more. "I can feel you squeezing me."

She could barely breathe, much less manage any kind of speech back to him.

But Devlin wasn't done. He held his body still as her climax rocked through her, but then he said, "Now we finish," before he switched their positions in a flash, securing her beneath him. He lifted her legs, putting them over his shoulders so that she was open even more to him. He thrust into her, driving into her core, and she shouldn't have felt another burst of pleasure.

But she did.

He thrust into her, moving in a fast and frantic rhythm, and all she could do was feel. Hold on tight in that wild ride and let the pleasure soar through her. It was as if her climax had never ended — maybe it hadn't. Maybe —

He shuddered against her. Devlin kissed her deep and hard and she could feel his cock jerking inside of her with the force of his release. His grip was tight, but not painful. He was holding onto her as if he never wanted to let her go. And she could taste the pleasure in his kiss. That heady euphoria. The rush she didn't want to end.

Julianna wished that she could see his face. She remembered what he'd looked like before, back at the house, when his blue gaze had gone blind with pleasure. The sight had taken her breath.

No, he'd done that.

Very slowly, he withdrew from her. She didn't move. Julianna was pretty sure she never wanted to move again.

A few moments later, he was back. Gently, he smoothed a warm cloth over spots that were starting to feel a wee bit achy, in a good way. When he started to rise again, Julianna caught his hand. She should be careful now. The hard desire had been satisfied. They should both go their separate ways. They should—

He climbed back into the bed with her.

His arms slid around her as he pulled her against him, cradling her.

Julianna didn't speak. Neither did he.

Screw what they *should* do. Julianna's eyes began to close. For that night, she'd stay with him.

CHAPTER TEN

"Drink your wine."

She had a wine glass in her hand. Julianna was back at home — Jeremy's home. She stared down at that wine, then up at Jeremy's handsome face. Who knew evil could look like a GQ ad? She did, now. "I'm leaving." Her fingers curled around the stem of the wine glass.

A smirk twisted his lips. "Leave…and your darling little sister will get her ass thrown in jail."

Julianna shook her head. "I won't let you do that." Not to Carly. She'd protect her sister. There had to be another way. Ethan had said they'd find a way. That he would help her.

Jeremy laughed at her. "Let's see you try and stop me."

She drank that wine. Not because he told her to do it. Not because she liked it. But because she needed a little liquid strength. "No." Her voice was firm. "Let's see you try and stop *me*." Because she was done letting him control her. Done with the pain and the horror and the shame that rolled through her. She'd mistaken a monster for a man. But the time for regrets was long gone. "I'm leaving you. My bags are packed and I—"

Jeremy was laughing again. She hated the sound of his laughter. So self-assured. So arrogant. "Oh, sweetness. You're not going any place. Soon, you're not even going to be able to stand, much less leave me."

Another threat. When would he see that she was serious?

She turned from him and headed for the door. Only the door seemed so far away.

His arm wrapped around her neck, jerking her back against him. "You think I'd let you publicly humiliate me like that?"

Her glass fell to the floor.

"I don't even know what the fuck it is about you…" His breath blew against her cheek. "Obsessed. Fucking obsessed. There's one way to deal with an obsession." Then he yanked her around to face him.

Only…his face was blurry. It shouldn't have been. Not with only one glass of wine.

He kissed her. Hard. Rough. She could taste blood and knew that he'd busted her lip. She tried to push against him, but it seemed to take so much energy just to lift her hands.

"Stop fighting."

She felt the sharp edge of a knife under her chin.

"Should've worked faster…I gave you more than enough to take you down…"

Enough what? And why couldn't she see him clearly?

"I am fucking obsessed with you, and that's a weakness. I won't allow for any more weaknesses."

She didn't dare move, not with the knife so close.

"It's time for you to understand who's in charge here, sweetness. I have the power. *Me*. Not you."

Anger burned through her, pushing back some of that strange numbness that she felt sliding through her limbs.

"And tonight, you won't be sleeping alone. Not tonight, not ever again. I married you, I own you."

She shook her head. Did the blade prick her skin?

"And I'm going to fuck you. I gave you some time, why didn't you appreciate that shit? I figured you'd come back to me, begging to get in my bed."

He was crazy.

"You were supposed to offer yourself to me." In his dreams.

"But you didn't, so I'm just going to take whatever I damn well want now."

She shoved at him, as hard as she could. Startled, Jeremy stumbled back.

"Leaving…you…" Why were her words slurred?

He'd dropped the knife. She picked it up and almost fell over when she did. No, she *did* fall. Julianna realized she was on her hands and knees, trying to crawl. Everything felt funny and the room was tilting.

But she still had the knife. It was her protection.

"You bitch." His hands closed around her hips. Jeremy heaved her around to face him. "You don't fight me, I'll kill—"

She shoved the knife at him. It sank into his chest. There was a wet, sloshing sound. A terrible, terrible sound. His eyes widened. Shock was there because he hadn't expected her attack. But he wasn't going to hurt her again. She'd kill him first.

Julianna pulled the knife out of him. Jeremy's hand rose, covering the wound that poured blood. She tried to scramble back, but couldn't. Her lashes were sagging, too heavy now.

Why did she feel that way?

Her tired gaze slid to the wine glass on the floor. She remembered his words. Had he said he'd given her something? Had he *drugged* her?

"Sweetness…" Jeremy grabbed for her again.

And she stabbed at him with the knife.

***

"Julianna!"

Her eyes flew open. She couldn't see anything at first. It was too dark, just like before…when she'd had red wine and a knife. Julianna swung out with her fist, punching and hitting as she fought for her freedom.

A man was swearing and reaching out for her.

She hit him harder and knew that she was fighting for her life. She knew —

Light flashed on. Light from a lamp on the bedside table.

Julianna blinked against that light, then she scrambled from the bed. Totally naked, she ran toward the bathroom, but then she froze.

I'm not at home. Jeremy isn't with me.

She risked a glance over her shoulder. Devlin was in the bed. He hadn't moved to follow her. His hand was still out, near the lamp. As she watched him, his hand rose and rubbed under his left eye. A red spot was already forming there.

I hit him?

"I'm guessing that was one hell of a nightmare," Devlin murmured.

Goosebumps covered her body. No big surprise considering the fact that she was standing there, stark naked, in the middle of the bedroom.

Devlin slid to the edge of the bed and stood. Julianna instantly tensed.

"Easy." He lifted his hands in front of him. "I'm not going to make the mistake of touching you again. Just take it easy, okay? When you want me to touch you, say it. And if you want me to keep standing the hell back, I can do that, too."

She didn't know what she wanted right then. She'd had nightmares before, plenty of terrible dreams since Jeremy's murder. But those dreams usually faded when she woke and Julianna had just been left with a dark, gnawing fear inside of her.

This time, things were different. This time, she hadn't forgotten. This time...

I think I'm the killer.

What had brought the memories back? Heather's attack? All of the fear she'd felt recently? One of the dozen shrinks she'd spoken to after being arrested had told her that her memories of that night *could* come back, provided she had a strong enough trigger.

The cops had wanted to lock Julianna up from the beginning. The Press had said she was guilty. But she'd been so sure that someone else must have come into the house and murdered Jeremy.

Sure, the evidence had shown her prints on the knife. Jeremy's blood had been on her clothes but...

But I thought there had to be another explanation.
She'd thought wrong.

"I'm sorry," Julianna told Devlin. Her lips felt numb. No, her whole body did.

He frowned at her. "For what?"

"H-hitting you." She'd been fighting blindly. She'd never meant to hurt him, but she had.

"Forget it." He didn't come any closer, but his eyes were blazing with emotion. "You were having a nightmare."

Julianna shook her head, then she stopped, realizing just what she'd nearly confessed.

"You *weren't* having a nightmare?" Devlin asked, cocking his head to the side.

No, the past wasn't a nightmare. It was reality.

She grabbed for her clothes. She could feel the weight of Devlin's gaze as he stood there watching her. Watching, but not touching. Keeping his word.

In seconds, she was dressed. She wondered if he saw the tremble of her fingers. Julianna knew she had to tell him something. She couldn't just run off in the middle of the night.

She also couldn't just stay there.

"I'm sorry," she said again.

"Julianna…"

"I have to go." She had to figure out what to do. Spending the rest of her life in a jail cell wasn't an option she wanted, but lying and hiding the truth? Could she do that forever? She turned for the door.

"Don't." The one word was bit out.

Her shoulders stiffened. In that moment, Julianna couldn't look back at him. "You don't really know me, Devlin. You know what you see, but that's just surface. You should stay away from me." He didn't need to get pulled down into the mess that was coming. If she went to the cops, *when* she went to them, the media would be all over her.

If Devlin was with her, they'd tear into his life, too.

He didn't need that hell.

"Where are you going?" Devlin asked her. She heard the hiss of a zipper behind her. He must have put on his jeans.

"Home." The home she hated. But it would have to do, for the time being.

"And how are you getting there? Dammit, let me help you! You hired me to—"

"I don't need a bodyguard any longer. My stalker is in jail." She had to get away from Devlin. If she told him the truth, no, she didn't want to see the way he'd look at her. He'd worked hard to get away from the crimes in his past. "I'll call a taxi, and I'll be fine."

"You're *not* fine."

No, she was shaking apart on the inside. "Good-bye, Devlin." Because it had to be good-bye. She wasn't any good for him.

She was a killer.

Julianna walked out of that bedroom and left him behind.

***

What. The. Fuck?

Julianna had left him. No, not just left, but straight up run from him. In the middle of the damn night. She hadn't even looked at him. When the cab had arrived, she'd rushed outside and that had been it. No more good-byes, no more nothing.

Devlin stood outside, watching the tail-lights of that taxi as it disappeared. He was still in his jeans and the t-shirt he'd grabbed and snow fell down on him. His toes were quickly growing numb out there, but he didn't care.

Something was wrong with Julianna. Very, very wrong.

She'd been on fire in his arms just two hours before. She'd been warm and trusting in the aftermath, holding him close, letting down all of her defenses.

He'd slept with her in his arms, and he'd felt more at peace right then...hell, he'd had more peace in those moments than he'd had in too long to remember.

Her voice had woken him. A fitful whisper. *"Leaving you…"* He'd understood those words. Then she'd muttered something else. Something about her bags. Had she said they'd been packed?

The tail-lights were gone now. He turned and headed back into his house. His first stop was his computer, and he pulled up every single file he had on Julianna…and on Jeremy Smith's murder.

Yes, the cops had found her with the deceased bastard. Julianna had been unconscious when the police arrived. She'd had her husband's blood on her. The murder weapon had been near her right hand.

He typed in a few passwords that he shouldn't know, and a few seconds later, he was staring at crime scene photographs.

Devlin pressed closer to the screen as he studied the photos. There was a wine glass on the floor. Very close to the dead body. Only the top of that wine glass had been smashed. The carpeting was damn lush in that room, he'd seen it for himself. It would take more than just a stray tumble for that glass to shatter that way.

He zoomed in on the picture. Jeremy Smith had been stabbed thirteen times. That much violence sure took one hell of a lot of rage.

"*Leaving…you…*" Julianna's voice whispered through his mind once more.

According to her own signed statements, Julianna didn't remember anything that happened that night, not after she'd been given a glass of wine by her husband.

The wine was gone. Not spilled on the carpet with that smashed glass. Gone.

Did he drug her?

But…

Devlin couldn't help but wonder, had Julianna remembered more? Remember something else that had scared her? Because he knew she'd been afraid. She'd fought him so desperately in that bed, damn near breaking the heart he hadn't realized he'd had.

"*Don't hurt me…*" A plea she'd made even before her eyes opened.

Jeremy had hurt her, though. Again and again.

Devlin pulled out his phone. He hesitated, then called the one person he thought could help. His call was answered on the second ring. Devlin didn't identify himself. He just said, "Julianna needs you."

***

She'd had the cab just…drive for about an hour. An hour while she sat huddled in the back, trying to get up the nerve to return home. But, finally, Julianna had realized she couldn't hide any longer.

She'd finally gone home. The cab pulled away even before Julianna opened the door to the Smith estate. She twisted the key in the lock and then turned the knob. The cold had her teeth chattering as she hurried inside. She turned off the beeping alarm and reached for the lights.

"You shouldn't be here."

The voice came from the darkness behind her. Far, far too close. She started to whirl toward that voice, but hard hands grabbed her and shoved her forward, banging her head against the nearest wall.

She hit hard, but Julianna didn't stay down. *Not again. Not ever again.* She gripped her keys between her fingers, turning them into sharp weapons, and she lunged up, whirling toward her attacker. She drove the keys at him just as hard as she could.

He swore and jumped back. It was so dark, she couldn't see where he'd gone. The looming shadows stretched everywhere she turned. "Stay away from me!" Julianna yelled, lunging out with her keys. But she just hit air and—

Laughter. Cold chilling laughter came from the darkness.

"You weren't supposed to be here," that low voice rasped. "You were supposed to be with the new lover. But since you *are* here…" He lunged from the darkness and slammed into her. She drove her keys at him and heard his howl of pain, but he grabbed her wrist, her right wrist and twisted.

She screamed as agony shot through her.

"Still weak, isn't it?" He had her pinned against the door. They'd crashed back into the wood. "If I apply just a little more pressure, I bet it'll break again."

She froze.

"Like I was saying…" He laughed. "Since you're here, I can go ahead and get rid of you now."

He's going to kill me.

She had no idea who the guy was or why he was in her home — or why he was going to kill her, but she wasn't going down easily.

He had her right wrist locked in his hands, but her legs were free, and he should be paying more attention to them. *Your mistake.* As hard as she could, Julianna drove her knee into his groin. His hold tightened on her wrist — tightened and *snap*.

She felt the bone break even as he howled in pain once more and stumbled back. She tore away from him and ran — not out the front door because he was right there. She ran into the nearest room, the den. She slammed the door. Threw the lock and hit the light switch. As the bright light flashed on in that room, Julianna dragged the closest piece of furniture over to block the door. The furniture she grabbed was a big, sturdy leather chair. Jeremy's favorite chair. She heaved and pushed and—

The door shuddered beneath the powerful boom of her attacker's fists. "You bitch!" He yelled. "Open this damn door!"

The hell she would. If she opened that door, Julianna knew she was a dead woman. With her left hand, she managed to yank out her phone. Her right hand was limp, useless, and pain radiated from her wrist.

The whole door shook. "Open. The. Door!"

"*Nine-one-one…*" A voice answered on the other end of the line. "What is the nature of your emergency?"

The door cracked.

"There's a man in my house!" Julianna yelled, wanting the bastard out there to know she was calling the cops. "He attacked me—hurry, hurry get here—"

Silence. The door had stopped shaking. A long crack slid from the middle of the door all the way to the top. The sound of Julianna's heaving breaths filled the room.

"Ma'am?" The operator said, voice sharp. "Ma'am, are you still with me?"

She was, for the moment. Julianna rattled off her address. "I don't hear him now." She inched toward the door. "Maybe he's gone."

"Ma'am, I have police personnel en route." A pause. "Are you in a secure location?"

That crack in the door was so long.

"I-I think so." She leaned closer to the door, straining to hear the sound of footsteps or *anything* on the other side. "I think he's gone. It's so quiet now and—"

"You fucking bitch…" A low snarl, one that she almost thought she'd imagined. "I'm not done with you."

Then…footsteps. Rushing away. The sound of the front door opening. The beep of the alarm.

"Ma'am?" The nine-one-one operator prompted. "Are you all right? Are you safe?"

Julianna shook her head. No, she wasn't safe. Heather was locked up but whoever that man had been…he'd wanted to kill her. She was as far from safe as it was possible to get. "Please hurry," Julianna whispered and then she put the phone down. She left it on because weren't you supposed to do that? Always keep the line open or something? But she needed a weapon so she backed away. Her gaze flew to the bar. All of the wine was gone—the cops had confiscated all of the drinks there during their investigation, when they'd been testing everything to see if she might have been drugged.

And no drugs had turned up in the wine bottles.

But glasses were still there. Julianna grabbed one of the wine glasses and she slammed it into the side of the bar. The crash of the shattering glass chilled her. She held up the jagged edge of the wine glass, struck by a sense of déjà vu. There was something so familiar about it…

Her fingers tightened around the stem. If that man came back, if he got through the door, he'd be the one bleeding.

Just as Jeremy had bled. Right in this room. Just a few feet away.

She couldn't suck in a deep enough breath. Couldn't calm her racing heartbeat. Nausea swirled in her stomach, probably from the pain of her broken wrist or maybe just from the terrible, gut-wrenching fear that she felt.

She could almost convince herself that she wasn't alone in that room. That Jeremy's ghost was there, laughing at her.

Laughing, the way her attacker had laughed. That cold, chilling sound.

The alarm was still beeping. No, *shrieking* now. How much longer would it be before the cops arrived? How much damn longer?

CHAPTER ELEVEN

Julianna's front door was wide open, and the shriek of the mansion's alarm blared into the night. Devlin ran up the steps and into the dark house. "Julianna!" he roared as fear closed around his heart like a cold fist. "Julianna, where are you?" After he'd made his phone call, uncertainty had gnawed at him. He'd just had to leave… he'd needed to make certain that she was safe. A phone call wouldn't have been enough. Devlin had needed to *see* her.

From what he could see right then, no, Julianna wasn't safe. Not at all.

"Julianna!" He hit the light switch. He'd seen it the last time he was there, a few feet away from the entrance. Illumination flooded the scene. The first thing he saw was the keys. They were just tossed on the floor. He frowned at them — *the keys meant Julianna was there* — then his gaze shot around the house.

When he saw the door, a door that appeared to have been fucking pounded by someone, his heart seemed to stop. "Julianna!" This time, her name was a roar as he raced to that door — the door that he knew led into the den. He grabbed the knob, but it was locked. "Julianna, are you in there?" He lifted his leg and slammed his foot into the door, aiming for the lock and doorknob. He'd bust that damn thing down and get to her.

He heard sirens outside, the cry still distant but coming closer. He lifted his leg and kicked again and —

"Stop it!" Julianna's cry. High and desperate. "Leave me alone! The cops are coming! Just leave me *alone!*"

"It's Devlin." He stopped kicking that door. He put his hand on the cracked surface of the wood, wishing that he could be touching her. "Baby, it's me. Open the door for me."

"D-Dev?" Then there was a gasp and a thud.

"*Julianna*!" She was scaring the hell out of him.

The door knob turned and she swung open the door. She had a broken wine glass in one hand. She didn't reach out to him, just stood there, her body trembling. "He said I shouldn't be here."

He grabbed her in his arms and pulled her close. She was warm and soft and alive. "Baby..."

The sirens were getting closer.

"H-he could still be here." She pushed against him. "Come into the den with me. We'll lock the door again. We'll stay safe. He couldn't get to me." She was talking far too fast. "I locked the door and put Jeremy's chair in front of it. *He couldn't get to me.*"

Light spilled onto her face. He could see a bruise already forming on her forehead. "Julianna, it's okay." He reached for her right hand.

She screamed. The sound was sharp and desperate and pain-filled.

He jerked his fingers back as if he'd been burned.

"He broke it," she whispered as she looked down at her hand. "When I tried to fight him, he broke my wrist."

The sonofabitch was going to suffer.

"Come into the den with me." Julianna was almost begging now. "We'll be safe in there. He couldn't get to me." She kept repeating that and it was tearing into him.

Car doors slammed outside, and the swirl of police lights flashed through the house. "You're safe, baby. I promise," Devlin told her, keeping his voice gentle. "The cops are here, and if that bastard is still anywhere on the property, he *will* be found." He planned to call in Chance and Lex and they were going to search every inch of the place.

Two uniformed cops rushed into the open doorway. They had their guns up and they immediately pointed them at Devlin.

"Julianna Smith?" One barked. "You called for help—"

She still had the broken wine glass in her left hand. He noticed that the cops were eyeing it with concern. "A man was in my house," she said, her voice too flat now, as if all of her emotion had vanished. "He attacked me."

The cop on the right frowned at Devlin. "And who are you?"

Faith Chestang walked in behind them. "He's Devlin Shade, her bodyguard." Her gun was in her hand. "Though I've got to wonder…where the hell were you during the attack, Devlin?"

He'd been too far away. He should have stayed at her side. Shit, this was on him. "Her wrist is broken," he said, voice grim. "And I think she hit her head. She needs an EMT." No, a hospital was what she needed.

"Julianna…" Faith's voice actually sounded concerned. He knew she had a rep for being good with victims. "I'm going to need you to drop your weapon so that I can get you some help."

Julianna blinked, appearing confused, then she glanced at her left hand. Her fingers still gripped the stem of that wine glass. Very slowly, her hand opened and the broken wine glass hit the marble. It shattered, the sound too loud right then.

"That's one way to do it," Faith muttered, then she waved behind her. "We need medical attention in here! Now!" She closed in on Julianna. "Where is he?"

"I don't know." Julianna shook her head. "I locked myself in the den. He was trying to break in."

From the looks of that door, her attacker had come close to succeeding.

"But he stopped." Julianna stared down at her hand. "Maybe he heard Devlin's car coming and he ran."

"I got here just a few moments ago," Devlin told Faith, trying to keep his voice soft and non-threatening, too. Julianna seemed too fragile in that moment. As if she were on the verge of shattering, just like that wine glass. "The bastard could still be close by. There weren't any cars outside when I arrived. Maybe he's on foot. Maybe—"

"Get a search going!" Faith called to her team. "Search this house. Search the grounds. Let's find him, *now!*"

An EMT rushed through the doorway.

"I'll need a description," Faith said, before the EMT could reach Julianna.

Julianna's gaze rose as she stared at the detective. "I didn't see him. It was dark. He just...grabbed me."

Faith's lips thinned. "Height, weight, anything...you got ideas for those, right? I mean, he grabbed you so..."

"I think…he was around Dev's height," Julianna spoke slowly, as if remembering. "And strong, so strong, like Dev."

The EMT reached for her right wrist.

"It was broken before," Julianna explained as she shook her head. "He knew that. Told me it was still weak. That if he applied just enough pressure, he bet he could break it again." Her breath rushed out. "And he did."

Faith shot a fast glance toward Dev. He nodded, understanding the fear that he'd just seen in the detective's eyes. *This isn't a random attack. The guy knows Julianna. If he knew about her wrist being broken, shit, then he knows her very well.*

The EMT was leading Julianna out of the house.

"I'll have more questions!" Faith called.

Julianna looked so small as she was taken out. Devlin wanted to find the bastard and destroy him. He reached for his phone.

"Calling in backup?" Faith asked him as she holstered her weapon. "You don't think the DC cops can handle this?"

"I think *you* can handle just about anything," Devlin told her, and he meant those words. He knew Chance had worked closely with Faith back when his buddy ran the security for Hawthorne Industries. Faith had been an All-Star there, no doubt, but she'd left Hawthorne Industries after some kind of blow-up with the big boss, Will

Hawthorne. A man who was one serious force to be reckoned with in D.C. and in the whole freaking world. A man with too much time and too much power. "But I still want my team in here because this one is personal."

Faith looked over her shoulder. Julianna and the EMT had vanished. "Yeah, I was worried it was." Her gaze came back to him. "After that interrogation, I knew." She gave a low whistle. "Are you being careful here? I warned you—"

"She's a victim." He could see that. Faith had to see it, too. "And she needs us both." He started to push by her, but Faith caught his hand, stopping him.

"You weren't with her tonight."

No, and he should have been.

"Why not?"

Because she walked out on me. Something happened...something terrified her and made her run from me. "We thought her stalker was in custody. *You* and I both thought it. It seemed safe enough for her to be on her own."

Her hand slipped away from him. "Maybe Heather Aslo wasn't working alone."

He'd already thought the same thing. "She's not safe. Not until we find the bastard out there who did this."

"Well, then there's something you should know..." Faith leaned in closer and her voice dropped. "Heather talked to two men earlier tonight. Her lawyer, Harry Gibbs, and that reporter, John Reynolds. Now, the lawyer doesn't fit the description of the attacker. The guy's size is all wrong, but Reynolds…"

Devlin remembered the green-eyed, blond reporter. "He's my height."

"And pretty close to your build." She gave him a little salute. "I'll be questioning him, you can count on it, but I thought you might like that information."

He sure did. "I owe you."

"The VJS tab just keeps growing…" She headed toward the den and the other cops who were in the area.

"Faith!"

She turned back toward him.

"What about Heather Aslo's boyfriend? Hugh Bounty? Did your team find him?"

She shook her head. "He wasn't home and a canvas of his neighborhood turned up nothing. There's an APB out on the guy now."

"Then maybe he wasn't home because he was here." The guy was sure high on Devlin's suspect list. He was tied right next to the reporter.

"I already thought of that. This *isn't* my first case." Her eyes narrowed. "We'll find him. Don't worry, Hugh will be in my interrogation room by dawn."

Provided that the guy hadn't already gone to ground. An ex-military guy, Hugh might not have any trouble disappearing.

Devlin headed outside and he didn't draw in another deep breath until he saw Julianna. She was in the back of an ambulance, and two EMTs were working on her. With his eyes locked on Julianna, Devlin called Chance and put the phone to his ear.

Chance answered on the fourth ring. "Too late," Chance muttered, his voice groggy, "or maybe it's too damn early for this phone call."

A feminine voice murmured in the background. Devlin knew that would be Gwen Hawthorne. Chance's one-time client was now the guy's obsession. *No, it's not obsession, it's love.* Devlin knew just how Chance felt for Gwen — despite the desperate battles the guy had waged to control himself around her.

"I need your help," Devlin said.

"You've got it." An instant response, and just like that, the grogginess was gone from Chance's voice. "What's the problem? What can I do?"

He was still watching Julianna. "You know Julianna Smith is our new client…"

"Yeah, Lex told me all about her." A tense note had entered Chance's voice. "What's she done?"

"Nothing." His hold tightened on the phone. "She's not like…not like the media says. She was attacked tonight. Some bastard was waiting in her house."

Silence, then… "I thought her stalker was locked up. That's what Lex said. That it was the step-daughter."

Because that was what Devlin had told the guy. "A man came after her this time. I'm out at the Smith mansion and the cops are crawling all over the place." He exhaled on a rough sigh. "But I don't think they're going to find anything. And I'm not going to let that guy just keep running around, attacking her."

"Didn't I hear that Heather has a boyfriend? Maybe it's him."

It wasn't surprising that their suspicions were in sync. "Faith has an APB out for the guy." What Devlin wouldn't give to go one-on-one with that fellow in an interrogation… "Can you come out to the mansion and supervise the search of this area? Faith is here, and I know she'll share more with you than she will with me."

"I'll try my charm," Chance allowed. "But Faith only shares what she *wants* to share."

And she'd shared the reporter's name with Devlin. *I'll be chatting with that guy, very fucking soon.* "I need VJS to help me track down a reporter named John Reynolds. I want both him and the boyfriend—Hugh Bounty—found. Those bastards are both connected to Heather, and that woman has already proven just how badly she wants Julianna dead."

One of the EMTs jumped out of the ambulance. The EMT grabbed one of the back doors and slammed it. "Shit, I've got to go. They aren't taking Julianna away from me."

"What?" Chance's voice rose. "Who's taking her?"

He was running toward the ambulance. "Bastard broke her wrist and I think he gave her a concussion. He is damn well going to pay." Devlin hung up the phone and grabbed the second ambulance door before it could shut.

"Hey, buddy," the male EMT said, "you need to back away—"

Devlin ignored him and opened the door. Julianna was lying on a stretcher inside, but her head turned and she met his gaze. "I want to come with you," he said. Devlin tried to sound non-threatening, a hard task considering the rage that was pumping through him. He needed to stay close to her, until her attacker was caught. Her safety was his first priority.

No, she was his only priority.

The EMT grabbed his shoulder. "You need to step back—"

"Please," Julianna pleaded. "I need Devlin with me."

The EMT let him go. "You family?"

"Close enough," he muttered, not even caring about the lie as he bounded into the ambulance. He saw that they'd already put a brace around her wrist. His fingers brushed against hers as he settled in near her.

Julianna gave him a weary smile. "I think I need to hire you again." The ambulance cranked and the siren blared. Her smile slipped away. "I'm not safe yet."

No, she wasn't. He brushed back her hair, being extra careful not to touch the growing bruise on her forehead.

"I have to do what's right," Julianna whispered. "I'm sorry."

Why was she apologizing to him?

"I did it," she said.

He frowned and leaned closer to her. "Baby, I think you're confused." He glanced over at the female EMT who was monitoring Julianna. "Is she okay?"

The EMT hesitated. "She took a pretty hard blow to the head. She's got a concussion, and that can manifest in confusion and—"

"I did it," Julianna said again, her voice stronger. "I'm sorry."

He didn't understand. "Julianna, just relax. Whatever you did, we can fix."

A tear leaked from her eye. "We can't fix this."

He brushed away her tears. "For you, I can fix anything."

CHAPTER TWELVE

She had a new cast. A lovely blue one. And she had a concussion. The doctors were telling Julianna that she needed to stay in the hospital for observation, but she had someplace else that she rather desperately needed to be.

"Come on, Julianna," Devlin urged her. "Just one day."

He'd been with her during all of the poking and prodding. He'd been swearing furiously when her wrist was reset. His rage had filled the room, but during that very, very long swearing fit, he'd been stroking her hair — ever so tenderly — the whole time.

"I have someplace I need to be," she said as her fingers stretched a bit. She'd forgotten what the cast felt like. Cold at first, then heavier, seeming to lock down around her wrist so tightly as the material hardened. She lifted up the cast, staring at it. Whoever that man had been, he'd wanted to hurt her. Kill her.

"Give us a minute alone, doc," Devlin said.

She lowered her cast, frowning at him. "A minute isn't going to change my mind."

But the doctor was already fleeing, probably intimidated by the hard glint in Devlin's eyes. Then again, the doctor had been glancing rather nervously at Devlin since the swearing began.

The door shut behind the doctor.

She braced herself for whatever stay-at-the-hospital lecture Devlin had planned.

He closed in on her, stalking slowly. Her chin tipped up.

He kissed her. Softly. Tenderly. Then he—very gently—curled his fingers under her chin. "You pretty much scared the shit out of me."

Julianna blinked.

"When I got to that house and saw the door open like that…when I saw that fucking smashed door to the den..." His jaw hardened. "I was yelling your name, but you weren't answering me."

Because when she'd first heard that frenzied yell, she'd been terrified that it was her attacker. It had taken more than a few precious moments for the truth to sink in. *Not the attacker. It's Devlin.*

"There aren't many things that scare me. But tonight…*you* did it. Or rather, the idea of something happening to you, of someone hurting you…that got to me."

She didn't know what to say. Or maybe she was the one afraid then. Afraid to say the wrong thing to him.

"You're getting to me," Devlin rasped. "Making me feel things I shouldn't."

"Don't." Julianna pushed against his chest. He stepped back and his hand fell away from her chin. "Don't feel anything for me."

His eyes widened in surprise. "Why the hell not?"

Because I'm a killer. I'm about go to jail. "Maybe the stories were right about me. You're a good man, Devlin. You need to find someone good, too." She jumped off the exam table. Maybe her legs trembled a bit. Maybe Devlin had to lunge forward and grab her before she did a header into the floor.

No maybe about that.

"You are good, Julianna."

She should tell him. But just saying the truth, right there to him…she was afraid it would break her own heart. Because once he knew, Devlin wouldn't look at her the same way. Any growing feelings he had for her would turn into disgust.

Thirteen times. Jeremy was stabbed thirteen times.

"I need to get dressed," Julianna said, fighting to keep her emotions under control. "Then I'm leaving the hospital. I don't care what the doctors say."

"Why." Not a question, but a demand.

"Because I have to talk with Detective Chestang."

His hold tightened on her. "What are you doing?"

She shook her head. "You don't want to know. Not really." Then, even softer, "Don't make me say it. Not to you." *Don't make me do the one thing that will break us both.* Did he think she didn't feel that connection between them? She did. It was far too strong to ignore. Not just lust, but something far deeper.

She'd sworn never to let another man get close to her. But she'd broken that vow. Devlin made her feel and dream and need.

He made her need things she couldn't have.

"You can say anything to me. You think I'll judge you? You think I'll turn on you?" Devlin demanded.

"I don't want to find out." And that was the stark truth. She didn't want to see what he'd do in that situation. He was a good man, and she was damned if she'd be the one who made him cross that thin line that might lead him down a different path.

She grabbed her clothes and went into the bathroom. As quickly as she could, Julianna dressed in that little room. Her head was throbbing, nausea churned in her stomach, and the cast was bulky as hell, but she pushed through all that. Julianna didn't glance toward the mirror, not even once. She just didn't want to look at herself.

Moments later, she was done. She opened the door and found Devlin standing on the other side of that hospital room. Her shoulders tensed as she braced herself for another argument from him, but Devlin shook his head.

"You want to go and see Faith? Then I'll take you."

"Thank you." She crossed to his side.

His blue eyes seemed even brighter. "I don't like this." Then he leaned close to her. His fingers feathered over her cheek. "I want to take you away from here. Get you as fucking far from this mess as I can."

Did he think she hadn't already had the same thought? *Run. Hide. No one will find me…not if I run far enough and fast enough.*

But there were some sins that you couldn't hide from. And some that you could never outrun. "It would have been nice," Julianna told him quietly, "if I'd met you before Jeremy." Before she'd learned to fear a man's anger so much. Before she'd learned to fear the darkness in herself.

What would it have been like? She was sure the attraction between them would have been just as fierce. But there would have been no secrets. No lies.

Just their need.

"You know me now," Devlin told her. "That's what matters. And I don't care what you have planned, I *won't* let you be in danger. I won't let you get hurt."

Oh, Dev. "You can't control everyone or everything." She leaned up and put her mouth against his. Her lips pressed lightly to his, and she just savored him a moment. This would probably be their last kiss, so she'd enjoy it.

And she'd remember him. "Thank you," Julianna said.

Then she pulled away. It was time to pay for her crimes.

They headed into the hallway, and Julianna nearly ran straight into the tall, blonde woman who was rushing toward her room.

"Julianna!" Avery's breath rushed out in surprise. Her wide eyes swept over Julianna's body. "You're...I heard about the attack. I wanted to check on you."

Check on her? Since when did Avery care?

Devlin moved to her side. "Now isn't the best time."

"I heard the house is destroyed." Avery's lips trembled. "Jeremy loved that house, and now it's broken."

Julianna felt pretty damn broken right then.

"Who did it?" Avery demanded. "Did you see the man?"

Julianna shook her head. "No."

"We'll get him," Devlin vowed. "Don't worry about that." Then he was steering Julianna around Avery.

"I'm sorry!" Avery cried out.

Julianna glanced back at her.

"I...loved him." Avery's shoulders sagged. "I think that...made me a little crazy for a while."

Julianna didn't know what to say to the other woman.

"You should have just let him go," Avery said and her gaze hardened on Julianna. "Because you didn't love *him*."

I wasn't the one keeping him prisoner. "You didn't know him, not nearly as well as you thought." Her fingers brushed against Devlin. "Let's go." Because she had a confession to make, one that she couldn't put off, not any longer.

"*I loved him,*" Avery's words followed her.

Julianna kept her spine straight. *And I killed him.*

***

Sophie Sarantos was waiting for them at the police station. When Devlin saw her, some of the tension finally left his body. Sophie knew how to handle her clients. She'd rein Julianna in. She'd stop her from doing—well, whatever the hell it was Julianna seemed so intent on doing.

Sophie hurried toward them. "You look like hell," she told Julianna.

Devlin frowned at her. Yes, Julianna was bruised but she was still fucking gorgeous. She'd always be.

"Let's go back to my firm," Sophie said as she cast a critical eye over Julianna. "I know a lot has been going on and I want to figure out who is—"

"Devlin called you."

He really didn't like the flat tone of Julianna's voice. The woman was worrying him.

Sophie cast a quick glance his way. "Last night," she allowed. "You'd left and he was…concerned for you." Sophie took a step toward them, moving easily in the spiky heels that she seemed to love. "He had a right to be concerned. You were attacked! I told you that you needed VJS for protection, and—"

Julianna walked around her. Sophie's mouth dropped.

"I thought my stalker was in custody." Julianna's voice drifted back to them. "I was wrong about that, too."

Sophie grabbed Devlin's arm. "What is she doing? You told me to stake out the police station, so I did. I've been here too damn long and I don't want any games."

Right. He had told her to be at the station— because he'd thought Julianna might head there after she left him last night. "Didn't Lex call you?" *And tell you to stop the police duty?*

"He did," she threw over her shoulder as she hurried up the steps after Julianna. "But I was checking sources here…and when they brought in Heather Aslo's boyfriend an hour ago, I wasn't about to leave."

Shit. "Hugh Bounty is here?" He wanted to get his hands on that SOB.

She didn't answer until they were inside the station. Inside and looking for Julianna.

"The cops brought him in," Sophie explained. "And the guy was *not* a happy camper."

He spied Julianna. She was leaning in close and talking with Faith. As he watched them, Faith put her hand on Julianna's shoulder and started leading her back to the interrogation area. *Hell, no.* "Julianna!"

She flinched and looked back at him.

Sophie double-timed it in her heels until she was right beside Julianna. "This is *my* client," she declared. "Just what is happening here?"

Faith shrugged. "Your client asked to speak with me."

The pounding of Devlin's heart seemed too loud. He held Julianna's gaze. There was no missing the fear there. *Don't do it. Leave with me, right now.* He wanted to say those words to her so badly because he knew, deep down, he *knew* what she was going to tell Faith.

It doesn't fucking matter.

"I'm sorry," Julianna told him.

He reached out to her and grabbed her hands. "She's confused," he bit out. "The doc said she has a concussion. She needs to go back to my place and rest, right now."

Faith frowned at her. "That knot on your head does look pretty—"

"No." Julianna straightened her spine. "We have to talk, now." She shook her head. "But you can't be there, Dev. Not you. *Please.* I can't do this with you here."

His chest burned. "Julianna…"

"It would have been nice, really nice, to meet you before…" Her smile was bittersweet. "But you're right. We do know each other now, and I'm very glad that we do. You are a man worth knowing. A man I won't forget." Then she turned and headed toward interrogation.

He took a step after her.

Faith's hand came down on his chest. "No way. You're staying out here." She jerked her head toward Sophie. "Her lawyer's coming in, but not you."

Faith turned and followed after Julianna. It was probably the first time she'd had to chase her suspect *into* an interrogation room.

"Stop her," Devlin said to Sophie.

She looked up at him. "What is happening here?"

"I think your client is making a confession."
He shook his head. "*Stop her.*"

Sophie took off at a run.

***

Julianna's hands wouldn't stop shaking. She
balled them into fists and sat at the little chair in
the interrogation room.

"Are you all right?" Faith asked and there
seemed to be genuine concern in the other
woman's voice.

Julianna nodded.

The door flew open. "My client needs a
doctor!" Sophie said, her voice hard. "This
meeting is over. Once she has rested and been
cleared by medical professionals—"

"I did it," Julianna blurted, then her
shoulders sagged.

Silence.

"My client is delusional," Sophie said. Her
high heels clicked on the floor. "Confusion is a
normal side effect from a concussion."

Faith lifted her brows. She crossed her arms
over her chest and stared down at Julianna. "You
delusional?"

"No."

"You confused?"

"I—"

Sophie put her hand on Julianna's shoulder. "My client has nothing else to say."

"Yes, I do." Julianna licked her lips. She kept her gaze on Faith. The detective had warm eyes. Kind eyes. "I remembered more."

Sophie's fingers tightened on Julianna's shoulder. "Stop."

She couldn't. "I remember being in the den that night. Jeremy gave me wine. I was—I was leaving him."

Sophie cursed. Very inventive curses.

"He wasn't going to let me go." *It's time for you to understand who's in charge here, sweetness. I have the power. Me. Not you.* Goosebumps rose on her arms as his words blasted through her head. "He told me...I knew he was going to rape me. He said he married me, so he owned me." She rubbed her chilled arms. "He'd tried before, to get me in his bed, but I slept in another room. I kept the door locked. He had a lover on the side, he told me about her..." The same day he'd broken her wrist, he'd told her about the other woman. A woman who'd kept him occupied when Julianna had tried to keep him the hell away. *What a fucking prince.* "So I thought he was just screwing her all those weeks. That he'd forgotten about me." She licked her lips. "He hadn't, though. That night, he wasn't stopping."

"I want you to listen to me," Sophie said, her voice seeming to fill that room. "You don't know what you're saying. You were attacked —"

"I think he put something in my wine." She'd told Faith that before, but none of the cops had believed her. "I remember being so woozy when he came at me. *He* had the knife. It was his. When he said he was going to fuck me, something snapped in me. I shoved at him, and he dropped the knife."

Silence. No, not a full silence. She could hear the steady ticking of a clock. Tick. Tick. Tick. The seconds were sliding by. Sophie wasn't trying to stop her, not anymore. "I was on my hands and knees. I had the knife. I couldn't walk…my whole body felt heavy. He-he grabbed me. Screamed that I couldn't fight him because he'd kill me." She looked down at her hands. The cast was so big.

"Julianna?" Faith prompted. "What happened next?"

"He wasn't going to rape me. He'd hurt me enough." Her gaze lifted again. "I struck out with that knife. He screamed when it cut him."

Tick. Tick. Tick. The clock seemed even louder.

"I pulled the knife out of his chest." Her breath came faster. "I tried to crawl away, but he lunged for me again." Her fingers flexed. "And I remember bringing up the knife…"

Tick. Tick.

"Did you drive that knife into him thirteen times?" Faith asked.

Julianna flinched. "I don't remember. I-I can't remember anything else."

Faith's eyes narrowed on her.

"Self-defense," Sophie said immediately. "This is an absolute clear case of self-defense. My client had to protect herself and she did the only thing that she could—"

Faith held up her hand, stopping Sophie. "You stabbed him twice, that's what you remember?"

She nodded.

"And his blood got on you when you stabbed him."

"Yes." She could see the blood soaking his shirt, dripping from the knife.

"You say you were drugged?"

Her gaze lowered to the surface of the table. The wood was old and scratched. "I think I was. I didn't feel...right."

"Maybe that was the rage. I've seen people snap. Go crazy with fury and everything around them seems different. They've told me the whole world was off when that killing rage hit them."

Julianna shook her head. "No, no, it wasn't that. I was *leaving* him." Killing him hadn't been her plan.

"Why then?" Faith moved closer. Julianna looked up at her. "You stayed with him for two months. Two months during which…you didn't sleep with him, but he hurt you. *Your* testimony. You stayed with him, you didn't flee. You didn't—"

"Victim blaming," Sophie snapped. "Faith, you are better than that."

Faith's eyelids flickered. "I know my victims. I know all about them. I know about women who stay with fucking psychos because those bastards have beat them down until they think they can't do anything else. I know about women who take hits again and again because they're protecting their kids, because they think staying with the monster is better than being alone on the street. I know women of every color and every income who live in fear because there's some fucking bastard out there swinging his fists…I know those women because my *mother* was one of them."

Julianna couldn't take her gaze off the detective.

Faith inclined her head toward her. "I saw the signs with you. The way you tensed when men came too close. The way you seemed to shrink into yourself when you were pressed too hard." Her jaw hardened. "And you know what my money is on? I think you stayed because you believed you were protecting someone else. Just who were you protecting, Julianna? Who was it?"

"I—" She shook her head.

A knock sounded at the door. Faith turned away. Marched to the door.

"If you want to stay out of a jail cell," Sophie whispered in Julianna's ear. "Let me do my job. Stop, for the love of God, just *stop* talking."

When Faith opened the door, a young, uniformed cop stood there. He handed Faith a manila file. She opened it and thumbed through the contents in silence. After a while, she sighed and said, "This changes things." She looked up and focused on Sophie. "You'll be getting your own copy of this report soon enough. For now…" She headed back across the room and gave the file to Sophie. "So…just to be clear, we all know that ADA Eastbridge was batshit."

ADA Eastbridge? Why were they talking about him?

Julianna peered over at that file. She knew that Sophie had gone through hell with the ADA recently—because the guy had been stalking her.

"All of the ADA's cases are being re-examined," Faith continued. "And with that re-examination, well, I focused my energy on his most recent cases."

"*He destroyed evidence*," Sophie said as she read the report Faith had just given her.

Faith nodded.

"Sophie?" Julianna pressed. "What's happening?"

Sophie glanced up at her. "You *were* drugged. Eastbridge destroyed the original lab results, probably because he knew no jury would convict you for murder—you couldn't have been legally responsible. Jeremy gave you so much Zolpidem that I'm actually amazed you woke up at all."

Zol—what?

"A dosage that strong can kill." Faith's voice was grim.

"That bastard Eastbridge," Sophie snarled. "He destroyed evidence? Falsified reports? Why the hell would he—" She stopped and stared at Julianna in horror. "Because you were my client. Because if the real test results came out, there wouldn't be a trial. He wanted the trial. Wanted us together…Oh, Julianna, I am so sorry."

The throbbing in her head was getting worse. So was the nausea. "The wine…it was in the wine?"

"Your glass was shattered, but we examined the rest of the bottle. You were the only one who drank that wine. There was none in Jeremy's system," Faith explained.

Because why would he drug himself?

"Where did he get it from?" Sophie wanted to know. "There has to be a trail we can follow. Someone who—"

"His step-daughter, Heather, has trouble sleeping. Night terrors." Faith's lips curled in a cold smile. "I learned that last night. She was demanding that we give her the medication she needed. Her—"

"Zolpidem," Sophie finished.

Faith nodded.

The throbbing in her head was like a drum, banging and banging. Why wouldn't it stop? "Her drugs? But...but I...killed..." She tried to focus on Faith but black spots danced in front of Julianna's eyes. She put her hand to her head. "Something...wrong..." Julianna stood, but her legs felt funny. "Dev...?"

"*Julianna!*" Sophie yelled.

Julianna hit the floor.

CHAPTER THIRTEEN

"Don't even think of running…because I'd have you before you even made it to the door."

Julianna blinked, her dark eyes hazy with confusion.

"You're in the hospital," Devlin told her, "and you're staying here for the next twenty-four hours. Even if I have to tie you to that bed."

She looked at the bed. Frowned. Then looked back at him.

"You passed out at the police station. An ambulance brought you here." An ambulance he'd ridden in. They needed to get out of the habit of that shit. "You should have stayed here to begin with. You have a concussion. You don't get to play around with something like that."

Tears filled her eyes. Hell, no. "Don't do it," he snapped at her. "Don't you dare do that."

"They…told you what I did."

Her big confession. "You pissed Sophie off, that's what you did. When your lawyer tells you to stop talking, you should."

She shook her head, sending her blonde hair sliding over the pillow. "No, Devlin, you know—"

"That the bastard drugged you? Tried to rape you? Yeah, I know that." He sure hoped Jeremy Smith was spinning over a fiery pit in hell.

"That I killed him," she whispered as the machines around her seemed to go wild.

Then she stared at him with wide, desperate eyes. Waiting for—what? Him to storm out? He bent forward and brushed back her hair. "Calm down, baby. The stress isn't good for you."

"D-did you hear me? I said—"

"He drugged you. He was going to rape you. You defended yourself." He shook his head. "That's not cold-blooded murder. That's survival."

Her lower lip trembled, but she caught it with her teeth, stopping that movement.

"You think I don't know you've been living in a nightmare?" Devlin asked her. "You think I didn't see the signs? I know, baby. *I know*. And I wish that I could take away all of your pain. I wish that I could make every fucking thing better for you. I wish…hell, yeah, I even wish that I *had* met you before you got tangled up with Jeremy. I would tell you to stay away from that bastard. Maybe I'd even kill him myself."

She grabbed his hand. "No."

He stared into her eyes. Eyes that were open and on his. He could see the flecks of gold in her gaze. He'd been watching over her, for hours. Tensing with every little movement. And realizing that he was in far, far too deep with her. And if he was this bad now…what would it be like a year from now? Two years?

She'll have all of me. Even my soul.

"I would kill to protect you. I would eliminate any threat to you." He thought she needed to know that. "So you seriously think I'd judge you for surviving? That I'd turn away from you? The fuck, no. The fact that you fought to survive makes me…it makes me want you even more."

She shook her head. "I'm going to jail."

"No." Not happening. "Sophie is in a meeting with the district attorney now. He knows that Clark Eastbridge screwed the evidence, and in light of all the facts emerging…she thinks he'll want to get this case out of the public eye as soon as possible. You're the victim, Julianna. Not the deadly femme fatale."

"I'm not either one." Her gaze fell. "I'm just…me."

His fingers slid under her chin. "Things are going to get better now. Faith has Hugh Bounty in custody."

A furrow appeared between her brows.

"Heather's boyfriend," he told her. "The guy with the explosive's experience." The guy at the top of his suspect list for the car bombing *and* the attack at her home. What Devlin wouldn't give to get that guy alone...

Too bad the fellow was currently surrounded by a dozen cops.

"Why was he in my house?"

"He was looking for something. Faith told me the upstairs area of the estate had been trashed." He rolled his shoulders. "Maybe he thought he could steal some jewelry or some cash. I'm sure Heather gave him the full layout of the place, and when the cops arrived, the bedroom safe was open."

"He said I...wasn't supposed to be there."

Maybe the bastard knew I was guarding you.

"You're safe," he told her and those words were a vow. "I'm with you, Julianna, and I'm not going any place."

Her hand squeezed his. "You should. You should run from me."

Not happening. "Baby, I—"

A knock sounded at the door. Then, seconds later, the door squeaked open. A woman poked her head inside, a woman with pale skin, blue eyes, and long, red hair. She stared at Julianna with shock on her face and fear in her eyes.

"Carly?" Julianna tried to sit up. "You shouldn't be here. You—"

Carly stepped into the room. Then she ran to the bed. She grabbed Julianna and held her tight. "Ethan called me," she said. "He told me…I'm so sorry! This is my fault. It's all my fault."

Julianna curled her arm around Carly as Devlin watched the two women. So this was the step-sister. The one Julianna had sacrificed so much for.

"It should have been me," Carly said, squeezing Julianna even tighter. "*Me.*"

The machines were even louder, beeping even faster.

Devlin put his hand on Carly's arm and pulled her away from the bed. She frowned at him. "Who are you?"

"I'm—" Shit, how was he supposed to answer that? Julianna's lover? Her bodyguard? Both?

"He's a friend," Julianna said.

His brows snapped together at that response. He was more. Dammit.

"Carly, you shouldn't be here," Julianna said. "You don't want to get pulled into this mess. I told you when the DA first filed charges…*stay away.*"

Carly's body was tense. "You didn't tell me that you stayed with that bastard because of me! That he was blackmailing you! I'll go to the cops! I'll tell them—"

"Yeah, you're sisters," Devlin muttered.

Carly's brows wrinkled.

"You'll incriminate Ethan," Julianna said. "You'll destroy everything you've built."

"How is that different from what's happening to you?" Carly demanded. "It's not and—"

Julianna's cheeks were flushed. Her heart beat too fast.

"That's it." He caught Carly's wrist and dragged her from the room.

"Dev!" Julianna called after him.

He didn't stop. He pulled Carly into the hallway and shut the door behind them. "You don't do that."

She backed up a step.

Okay, shit, he should go easier. She was Julianna's family but...Julianna was *everything*. "She's got a concussion. The woman fucking hates the hospital as it is. She has to stay calm and you can't upset her."

Carly slid back another step. "Who are you again?"

"I'm the man with Julianna." He thought that said it all. "And no one is going to upset her, got it? So that means you don't talk about going to the cops right now." Had he seriously just said that? He had. "We clear this situation up, one problem at a time." He reached into his pocket and pulled out a VJS card. "Go talk to them. Ask for Chance or Lex. They'll get you taken care of until Julianna is out of the hospital."

Her fingers curled around the card. "Julianna told you...everything, didn't she?"

He stared back at her. "I'm not the cops. I'm—"

"The man with Julianna. Right." She tucked the card in her pocket. "I'm sorry." Her voice was quiet. Hushed. "If I'd known, I would have turned myself in. I never would have let her get hurt for me."

He believed her. "She was protecting you."

"Who protects her?"

I do. From now on, that would be his job.

He turned away and reached for the door.

***

Julianna has been hurt so much. Too much. Carly Shay hurried toward the elevator. The last thing she'd ever wanted was to hurt Julianna and now—

The elevator doors opened.

Carly rushed inside and she hit...someone. Warm, strong hands flew up and wrapped around her shoulders. "Excuse me," she said, glancing up quickly. "I didn't mean—"

Ethan. Ethan Freaking Barclay.

Carly tried to step back, but he pulled her closer. The elevator doors shut behind her, sealing her inside that too small space with him.

"Carly," he said and his voice was that perfect, dark temptation that she remembered. A temptation that she'd given into, once.

He was different now, though. The years had made him—harder? His face was sharper and his eyes were still that incredible gold, but they were glinting with angry emotion. Fury and—

"I guess the scars show I'm as twisted on the outside as I am on the inside," he told her.

Scars?

Her gaze slid over his face. Now she realized that he *did* have scars. Two slashes, one across each cheek. She'd been staring into his eyes—she'd never seen anyone else with golden eyes like his—and she hadn't even noticed those scars at first. "You aren't twisted," she said, the words coming before she even realized it.

But then, she'd always had a problem with Ethan. He made her want to do things, feel things, that she shouldn't.

And I shouldn't be here with him now. His touch was singeing her. She was reminded of the girl she'd been before. So wild and reckless.

Not the woman she was now. *Control. Control is key. Always.* Because if she lost her control, she'd lose everything.

"I knew you'd come for Julianna." He shook his head. His fingers slid down her arm in a caress, and then he let her go. "You two, you'd really do anything for each other, wouldn't you?" His hand shot out and he hit a button on the control panel. The elevator stopped.

"Do you know how many years it has been since I last saw you?" Ethan asked her.

She did. She knew the years. She knew the days. She knew the sleepless nights. Did he know that, once upon a time, she'd been in the psych ward, calling for him?

Control is key. "I haven't been hiding, Ethan. I've been working and living in New York. It was easy enough for you to find my number and call me—"

"When you were seventeen, I was ready to kill for you."

He *had* killed for her. He'd driven that knife in the last inch to end the life of the bastard who'd hurt them both so much.

"*You* saved us back then" Ethan said. A muscle flexed in his jaw. "I owed you for that. So I stood back and let you walk away."

She hadn't walked. She'd run. Full speed ahead.

"Am I supposed to let you do that again?" His hand lifted and slid under the curtain of her hair. "I missed you…"

His voice was so low. Maybe he hadn't actually said those words. Maybe—

He kissed her.

***

"Julianna!"

Her head snapped up at Devlin's cry. She was standing on the side of the bed, yanking at the cords that connected her to all of the machines and trying to fight her way to the door.

He ran toward her. "Baby, what part of taking-it-easy are you having trouble with?"

"I have to see Carly!"

"No. You have to get better. You have to worry about *you*." His hands curled around her. He lifted her up easily and sat her right back in bed. "You're staying here until the docs say you're clear. Carly is fine. She's going to VJS, and the team there will take care of her."

"She shouldn't be here. She needs to go back home!"

"No." He shook his head. "This is exactly where she needs to be. You aren't going to suffer for her ever again and her secrets—they're going to come out, sooner or later."

But he didn't know all of Carly's secrets. Even Julianna didn't know them all.

"Right now, my focus is on you. Your safety. Your life. *That's* what matters to me." He sat on the edge of the bed, caging her with his hands. He leaned in close. "What the hell do you think I felt like when they rushed you out of that interrogation room and you were unconscious?"

"I-I don't know."

His jaw hardened. "We need to get a few things straight."

She needed to get out of that hospital room.

"You matter to me."

Her brows shot up. He'd almost said those words like they were some kind of accusation.

"It happened too fast and I'm in way too deep with you, but you *matter*." His breath heaved out. "So, for me, will you *please* stay in bed until the doctor releases you?"

Her hands were against his chest. Her right hand — and the cast — rested over his heart. "What else do we need to get straight?"

He frowned at her.

"You said a few things," she whispered. "What else was there?" *You matter.* Did he realize just how much he was coming to mean to her? He kept learning her secrets and not flinching away. He was learning all about her — good and bad, mostly bad — but still standing steadfast at her side.

She hadn't planned to get involved with him. But sometimes, life wasn't about plans. It was about desires. Needs.

"No more running from me in the middle of the night. If demons chase you, come to me."

She stared into his bright blue gaze, unable to look away.

"Come to me," he said again, "because I'll be there for you, I fucking swear it."

***

The kiss was everything that it *shouldn't* have been. Hot. Wild. Consuming. The years fell away and Carly felt the same intense desire stir within her. A desire that had scared her years before…and still scared her then.

Carly jerked away from Ethan. Her fist hit the button on the control panel and the elevator started moving again.

"That's good to know," Ethan said. Confident, sexy Ethan.

She'd known him well years before. But now…now he was a stranger to her. *A stranger I shouldn't want.*

"Some things have happened in my life recently," Ethan said. "They've made me reevaluate a few things. You're one of those things."

Her laughter was bitter. Right. Like Ethan cared about her. Never had, never would. She knew he'd had a fiancée, had far too many lovers.

So *maybe* she did keep track of him a bit. And that stalker-shit wasn't healthy.

Ethan Barclay wasn't healthy. "I'm not here for you," Carly told him. The elevator doors opened. Thank goodness. "I'm here for Julianna. You need to stay away from me, and I'll do you the same courtesy." Because they were too dangerous together. Far, far too dangerous.

"I like your hair that color. Red looks good on you." He paused. "But then, almost anything does."

She whirled and headed out of that elevator. She was in the lobby and there were plenty of people around. All the better to run and hide. All the better to —

"Excuse me, miss?"

She glanced to the right. A tall, blond man was staring at her. He gave her a broad smile. "You...are Carly Shay, aren't you?"

"Who are you?" How the hell had he known her name? Worried now, she tensed.

"It's my business to know things," he told her. "My name is John Reynolds, and I'm a reporter for the DC Journal."

Nightmare. "I don't have anything to say to you."

"Really? Because I thought you were Julianna Smith's sister? I mean, step-sister."

She needed to get away from him. "I don't have time to talk. I have to go." She marched right past him.

He followed her. "I think she's in danger."

"What tipped you off to that?" Carly demanded. They were near the glass exit doors. "Her recent trips to the hospital? The car bomb?" Ethan had told her about that, too. He'd terrified her.

Julianna, you can't risk your life for me!

"Give me five minutes," John said. "And together, we can help your sister."

She stopped. The glass doors had automatically opened for her.

"The world thinks she's a devil right now. Let's change their minds. Let's make her safe again."

Oh, but the guy was a born manipulator. He probably made for one kick-ass reporter.

"Five minutes," John pushed. "That's all I'm asking for." He pointed to the right. "There's a cafeteria down there. We can talk there, with plenty of people around."

Her hesitation stretched a bit more. She owed Julianna.

"Give me her side of the story," he said. "Let's help Julianna."

***

What in the hell was Carly doing? Ethan watched her as she talked with that ass-bite reporter, John Reynolds. Why was she standing so close to the guy? Why was she talking to the leech?

Carly shook her head and turned, striding out of the glass doors.

Good. Ditch him.

But John Reynolds rushed right after her.

Ethan's eyes narrowed. That reporter prick was going to be a problem. It was a good thing that he was so skilled at eliminating problems.

CHAPTER FORTEEN

"What the hell do you mean…the cops let Hugh Bounty walk?" Devlin paced in front of his fireplace, his body filling with fury. "When did he get out?"

Devlin and Julianna had only been at his place for a few hours when he'd gotten the phone call from Lex—a call that was not putting him in the best of moods. After twenty-four hours, Julianna had been given the all-clear to leave the hospital. He'd thought she'd keep relaxing at his place, then he'd learned this shit.

"He had an alibi? Some drunks at a bar? Hell, no, I don't buy it. You know your friends will always cover for you. His drinking buddies could be spouting BS." He raked his hand through his hair. "You've got eyes on him, though? You'll let me know where he goes?"

He heard the floor creak behind him and Devlin glanced over his shoulder. Julianna was there, staring at him with wide eyes.

"Good," Devlin told Lex. "Don't let him out of your sight. I want to have a one-on-one chat

with the bastard. I'll be there soon." He shoved
the phone into his pocket.

Julianna walked toward him. "Let me guess.
Heather's boyfriend is out?"

"Heard that, huh?"

She nodded.

"He had some friends alibi him. Faith held
the guy as long as she could, probably hoping her
uniforms would turn up more evidence to tie him
to your attack, but there was nothing." Nothing
they had found. But VJS wasn't done. *Now it's our
turn.* "Lex followed the guy to a bar called Fast
Shots."

She glanced toward the window and the
bright sunlight. "Little early for a drink, isn't it?"

"Not if you've spent too many hours in
interrogation. The guy will be looking for a
release. Maybe he'll get drunk and talk too
much." He lifted a brow. "I've seen that shit
happen plenty of times."

"You mean you want him to talk too much,
to you." Her head tilted. "You're going to meet
with him, aren't you?"

"Your car exploded into a million pieces. A
fellow who happens to be an explosives expert
has been sleeping with the woman who took a
shot at you." *Faith, you'd better keep Heather locked
up.* "Hell, yeah, I'm planning to talk with him."

"Right." Her shoulders straightened. "Then
so am I."

"Um, the hell, no."

Her eyes turned to slits. Seriously angry slits. "The last time I checked," Julianna said, "you were working for me."

She hadn't just said that. He took a step toward her. That cute chin of hers notched up. "Baby, I'm not accepting a damn dime from you."

"Your business is not going to last long at that rate."

His lips twitched. Dammit. She needed to stop being both hot and cute. "I can take care of my business."

"And I can make my own decisions. No one else is ever going to control me again."

Oh, hell, he hadn't meant… "I just want you safe."

Her expression softened. "And I don't want you running into trouble for me. If this guy is the one who attacked me, then I think I deserve to be there to question him."

She had a point. It wasn't a *safe* point though, so he hated to admit it. *Is it so fucking wrong that I want to wrap her up and protect her from everyone and everything?*

Maybe. But that was just how he felt.

"When we talk to him," Julianna continued, "maybe he'll give something away. Maybe his voice will click and I'll *know* he's the one who was in my—in Jeremy's house."

Another point. Damn. "Fine," he gritted out. "But we stay together, the whole time, got it?"

She smiled at him. Such an innocent, angelic smile. One that made him nervous. "I never had any other plan."

He didn't buy it. The woman was planning something right then. "You need to start trusting me."

Her gaze darted to the floor, then back up to his. "I do."

He shook his head. "No, baby, completely trusting me. Believing that I won't sell you out. That I won't turn my back if I learn something about you that isn't one hundred percent fucking good." He strode past her and grabbed his coat. "You should count on me." He shouldered into the coat. When he glanced back at Julianna, she was staring at him.

One of those deep, intense stares that could make a man nervous.

"In the beginning…" Julianna's voice was mild. "When I first went into your office…if I'd told you then that I had killed Jeremy, what would you have done?"

His teeth snapped together. "This isn't the beginning," he growled.

"You would have turned me in to the cops, right?" She tucked a lock of hair behind her ear. "I knew that. Why do you think I'm the one who went to Faith? Why do you think I didn't tell you first?"

"Julianna—"

"Because I could see that you were changing. I was changing, too. Wanting things…that I shouldn't. Part of me did want you to say, 'Screw it. Guilty or innocent, I still want you.'"

I do.

"But that wouldn't be right. Because a man like you shouldn't want a killer."

She was so wrong. "You're not a killer." She was a survivor. In many ways, they were so alike. Did she think he truly didn't have a darkness inside? Living, breathing, growing?

She just smiled a sad smile.

"You're not," he snapped.

She walked past him.

"Uh, Julianna?"

"Fast Shots is waiting, and for the record, I could really use a drink right now."

Swearing, he hurried after her.

***

Fast Shots was truly a hole in the wall. Dark and musky, the place looked as if it had seen many, many better days. And those days had been long ago.

Even though it was early, there were a few people in the bar. Three men. Two women.

"Which one is Hugh?" Julianna asked as she narrowed her eyes. She'd never met Heather's lover before but...

If I were looking for a guy who was big, like the jerk who attacked me, I'd pick that guy over by the bar. The blond who was downing shots as fast as he could.

"That one," Lex Jensen said, pointing toward the bar and the blond shot-drinker.

Lex had been waiting outside and when they'd arrived, he'd gone in with them. She knew that Lex was rather heavily involved with Sophie. From what Sophie had said, they were serious. And happy. A rare combination.

"How are we going to play this?" Lex asked. "Are we—shit, man, wait!"

Devlin wasn't waiting. He was already marching across the bar. Lex rushed after him and so did Julianna. Her hip bumped into a nearby table as she hurried forward.

Devlin grabbed Hugh's shoulder and spun the guy around. Hugh's shot glass went flying.

"What. The. Fuck!" Hugh snarled and shot to his feet, fists clenched. "Who the hell are you?"

Her heart slammed into her chest. Hugh was as big as Devlin and definitely as muscled. Maybe even a little more so. There was a whole lot of rage flaring in his eyes. A *lot.*

Devlin smiled at him. "I'm the guy who wants to kick your ass."

"Here we go," Lex muttered, running a hand through his hair. "And Dev thinks I have control issues."

Her gaze swung between the men. Was Hugh the one who'd attacked her? She didn't know for sure. He was the right size but...

Hugh slammed his hand into Devlin's chest. "Get the hell away from me."

Devlin didn't move an inch. "You're Heather Aslo's lover."

Hugh's eyes squinted. "I was, but now the dumb bitch is in jail." He motioned to the bartender. "Another round." Then his gaze — a hard green — cut toward Lex and Julianna. His stare lingered for a moment on Julianna. Then he grinned at her. "You're pretty. Want to go in the back and fuck?"

Her jaw dropped.

His grin stretched. "I'll give you a ride you won't —"

Devlin had him against the bar in an instant. He moved in a fast glide and shoved Hugh back hard enough to send more glasses tumbling to the floor. Even as Julianna blinked in shock, Devlin's fist was up and ready to pound into Hugh's face.

"No!" Julianna yelled. "Devlin, *no!*" That violence had erupted so fast. It was dangerous. Deadly.

Scary.

Devlin froze.

Hugh didn't. Hugh grabbed a bottle of whiskey and swung it toward Devlin.

"*Dev!*" Julianna cried out.

Dev ducked and the whiskey bottle missed him. Then he punched out. Once, twice, and the whiskey slipped from Hugh's fingers because the guy was howling and reaching for his now bleeding mouth.

Julianna backed up. Dev was...he was different right then. A heavy aura of rage clung to him.

"You don't fucking look at her," Dev snarled. "Do you hear me? You don't go near her. You don't touch her."

She retreated even more.

"Julianna?" Lex touched her shoulder. She flinched away from him. "Julianna, are you all right?"

Hugh was bleeding. Dev had just...pounded the man. Violence. She hated violence now.

And Dev—even his voice was different. So filled with fury and hate and jealousy.

She'd thought Jeremy was good at first. Then he'd changed, too.

Her head began to throb. She pushed away from Lex. She shouldn't have come. Dev had tried to keep her away, but she'd thought she might recognize Hugh's voice or his hands or *something*.

But she hadn't. Instead, she was just afraid.

Julianna spun and ran for the door. *I am so sick of fear. When will it ever end?* Why was she letting it control her so much? She shoved open the bar's door and hurried outside, gulping that cold air desperately as she tried to push through that suffocating fear. She was tired of being afraid. *Tired.*

"He won't hurt you."

The air was cold, and that was good. Her cheeks were burning hot. Julianna glanced over her shoulder and saw that Lex had followed her outside. He was standing a few feet away, studying her carefully. "You should be inside with Devlin," she told him. "He needs you for backup."

"Devlin doesn't really need anyone."

Doesn't he?

"He won't hurt you," Lex said again.

She glanced toward the street and the buzz of cars. "He just kicked a man's ass in about two seconds flat. I didn't…I knew he was strong, but I'd never seen—"

"It's not like we grew up easy," Lex said, his voice gentle. "We had to fight for what we wanted. In group homes, the older kids would make our lives hell. In schools, shit, you think it was ever easy being the kids that no one wanted?"

She turned toward him.

"You fought for what you wanted," he told her once more, giving a grim nod. "But you know what we never, *ever* did? What not one of us would do?"

She knew that "us" he spoke about was the family they'd created — Lex, Chance, and Devlin.

"We never hurt anyone weaker than us. We *never* hurt the innocent. The whole reason we started VJS was because we wanted to protect, not destroy."

The fear was fading. Slowly. "It's hard for me to trust — "

"I would trust Devlin and Chance with my life."

She shook her head. He wasn't getting it. "It's hard for me to trust *myself*. I'm the one who married Jeremy. I'm the one he manipulated. If I was wrong about him, how can I know that I won't be wrong about someone else, too?"

He watched her with his unfathomable green eyes.

"Go back inside," Julianna urged him. "Devlin needs you."

He turned to go, but then paused. "Have you seen the way the guy looks at you?"

She didn't know what he was talking about.

"If Dev needs anyone," Lex added, "it's not me." He glanced back at her and smiled. Oddly, though, his smile wasn't reassuring. It was scary. Dangerous. "I told you that Devlin would never hurt you, and I sure hope I can count on you for the same thing."

"What? I-I wouldn't hurt Dev—"

"You just looked at him like he was a monster. You walked away from him. It's not always fists that hurt."

Then he was gone. She stood out there, the cold sweeping around her. Deeper now, tighter, that cold clung to her. Julianna wrapped her arms around her stomach, being very careful with her broken wrist. She thought of men and lies.

Secrets.

And desires.

I don't want to be afraid any longer.

***

Julianna stood outside of Fast Shots, her gaze sweeping the street. She was the perfect target in that moment. No bodyguard was around to run and protect her. No cops were close to shield her.

Perfect.

Only...

She has what I need.

The file hadn't been at the Smith estate. It hadn't been there where it damn well should have been hidden. The only person with access to it *must* have been Julianna.

Jeremy Smith had been a straight-A bastard. He'd deserved a thousand deaths. Did Julianna think she was his first victim? Hardly. The psychopath had just been good at shielding his true nature…from all but those closest to him.

You hurt the ones you love. Wasn't that a saying? Or a song? Or some shit? But Jeremy Smith hadn't actually loved anyone. He'd just loved his power. His absolute control.

In the end, he'd had no control. No power.

Julianna had stayed with him for one reason—blackmail. Jeremy had loved using his "security consultant" Ray Holliwell for all of his dirty work. But without the big boss behind him, Ray had crumpled quickly. He'd spilled plenty about where the secrets were being kept.

Only now, Julianna had control of the files. She was the keeper of the secrets.

No, that shit isn't going to work. I am the one who gets the power now!

It had seemed like such a genius plan before. Julianna would be in prison and Jeremy would be in the ground. But now…things had changed.

Time for you to get in that damn ground, too, Julianna. Go join your husband.

CHAPTER FIFTEEN

Hugh laughed even as blood dripped from his busted lip. "Did you see the way she looked at you?" He shook his head. "Guess you won't be tapping that for a while."

Devlin could see himself grabbing the guy again and slamming Hugh's smirking face into the bar top.

Keep your fucking control. Because, yes, he had seen the horror in Julianna's eyes. She'd looked at him...*and had she seen Jeremy?*

"Jealousy." Hugh grinned. "Gets you every damn time."

The bastard had deliberately taunted him. Devlin could see that now. He could also see that Hugh wasn't just some brain dead muscle doing dirty work for Heather. *This guy is sly. He's playing me.* Had he played Heather, too?

"I ain't got anything to say to you," Hugh pointed to the door—a door that Lex was currently entering. "So you and your buddy can get your asses out of here. Before I get my buddy the bartender—" He paused and looked around, seeming to realize that the bartender was nowhere to be seen. "Before I get him to call the cops on you."

"Do it," Devlin invited.

Hugh swallowed. "Get the fuck out. Julianna Smith is a killer and if you're with her — you're obviously fucked in the head."

Don't pound his face in again. Don't. "Is that what Heather told you? That Julianna killed her step-father?"

"That's what every newspaper in the city says, man." He was still smirking.

Lex was only a few feet away now. Where was Julianna?

"I would have thought…" Lex drawled as he closed in. "That Heather would have been a bit glad her step-father was dead."

"Why?" Hugh demanded. "She loved that pompous asshole. She—"

"How did he control her?" Lex asked.

Devlin slanted him a fast glance.

"That was his thing, right? I mean, Julianna couldn't have been the first. And if Heather really was close to him…"

Hugh glanced away from them. "You ain't cops and I ain't talking anymore."

"Did he hurt her?" Devlin asked, wondering what the hell was happening there. Had Jeremy abused his step-daughter, too? Had he—

"Why would he hurt her? They were just the fuck alike. After what he did for her, she'd bleed for him." Then Hugh blinked, realizing that he'd probably said too much. "Get out. Get out *now!*"

Lex and Devlin surrounded him. "Not until you tell us...just what did dear old dad *do* for Heather?"

***

She saw him walking toward her on the sidewalk. Julianna's shoulders tensed and she glanced toward Fast Shots. John Reynolds was closing in on her, moving with a way too determined stride, and fleeing back inside the bar seemed like a good option.

Instead, she exhaled slowly and she held her ground.

"I figured," John said as he stopped beside her, "that if Hugh was here, you'd be close by."

She lifted a brow. "And why is that?"

"Because the guys from VJS probably think he attacked you." He glanced toward the door. "Are they in there, trying to *convince* him to talk?"

"What do you want?"

His gaze slid back to her. "I did a jailhouse interview with Heather Aslo."

"Wonderful for you." More cars buzzed past.

"I also talked with your sister, Carly Shay."

She didn't speak.

"Aren't you going to say that's wonderful for me, too?" He prompted, inclining his head toward her.

"Stay away from my family. Carly has *nothing* to do with the case against me." If Carly had told the reporter about the past, they were both screwed.

"She was very protective of you. A lovely woman, your sister," he added, musing a bit. "Beautiful, but fragile. I did a little research on her. Is it true she spent some time in a psych ward as a teen?"

She lunged toward him.

He put his hands up and quickly backed away. "Careful, your temper is coming out. Heather told me that you had a temper. She said that temper is why you and Jeremy fought so much. Fought so long and hard that her beloved step-dad had to restrain you. *That's* how you broke your wrist that time. You were swinging at him and he had to stop you. You seem to be a very violent woman." He paused. "At least, according to Heather."

"Heather tried to kill me. If you're looking for violence, look there." She had to get away from him. Talking to that reporter would do nothing but bring her trouble. She reached for the door to Fast Shots.

"I think she's lying," John called after her. "I think every word Heather told me was a straight-up lie."

She hesitated.

"Come with me, and I'll tell you why."

***

"Heather said her mom was a bitch," Hugh muttered. He'd grabbed a napkin and put it to his mouth. The white cloth turned bloody. "Always in her way, always getting all the attention, getting everything that Heather wanted."

Devlin and Lex shared a grim look.

"Then one day…" Hugh snapped his fingers. "Just like that, she wasn't in the way any longer."

"She died in a skiing accident," Lex recalled. "I pulled up the reports and—"

Hugh laughed. "Did she? Interesting, and here I thought the woman *never* skied."

Hell. "Jeremy killed her?" Devlin asked.

"I don't think the man liked to let go of the things he owned."

People aren't things.

"If you check, you'll see the first Mrs. Smith was consulting divorce attorneys right before that, um, accident."

"Sonofabitch," Lex rasped.

"Yeah," Hugh said, "he was."

Devlin braced his legs as he studied Hugh. "Where do you fit into all of this?" Because he was sure he was staring at the man who'd put a bomb in Julianna's car. Did that make Devlin killing mad? Hell, yes, it did.

"I'm innocent." Hugh shrugged. "Just a dumbass who fell for the wrong woman." His lashes flickered a bit. "How was I supposed to know she was crazy?"

"So you aren't jumping to Heather's defense?"

"Heather…" He tossed his bloody napkin onto the bar. "She isn't my problem anymore."

You're my problem, buddy.

Hugh tried to walk around him, but Devlin just blocked his path.

Hugh sighed. "Shouldn't you be chasing after that pretty blonde? You know, making sure nothing bad happens to her."

Devlin stiffened. "Did you just fucking threaten her?"

"I'm not the one you need to worry about. When her car went boom…" He made a little exploding motion with his fingers and his smirk returned. "I wasn't even in D.C. The police checked out my alibi. I was hanging with some army buddies, having some drinks and just enjoying life."

Did the guy think he was a fool? "You could have made the bomb before you left, then just given Heather instructions on how to place it in the car."

"I could have." He shrugged. "But I didn't."

Hugh stepped to the right.

So did Devlin.

"Seriously, get the hell out of my way," Hugh growled.

Devlin didn't move. "Were you at Julianna's house last night?"

"No."

"Did you *hurt* her?"

Hugh leaned in close. "I haven't touched your girl." He seemed to grit the words from between clenched teeth. "Now this is damn harassment. Leave me the hell alone." His shoulder slammed into Devlin's, but Devlin didn't hold the guy back this time. His arm slid down Hugh's side and he let the bastard walk right past him.

Lex whistled when the door closed behind Hugh. "That was a waste of time."

Devlin opened his hand. Hugh's phone was in his palm. "I wouldn't say that." Julianna wasn't the only one who knew a bit about picking pockets. He had a few skills in that area, too.

***

"Well, well…" Hugh drawled as he exited Fast Shots. "Isn't this cozy?"

Julianna looked away from John—and over at a still bleeding Hugh. He smiled at her. "You just find new friends every place, don't you?"

John stepped in front of her. "He's dangerous, Julianna. Don't get near him."

Hugh laughed. "That's right. I'm big, bad and far too fucking dangerous to know."

"I got access to your military records," John fired at him. "I know about the so-called *friendly* fire incident. About the explosion *you* set that took out three of your team-mates."

Hugh's laughter died. "You don't know shit."

"I know you're a man with some serious anger issues. You were pushed out of the army because they thought you were too much of loose cannon—a real powder keg that liked to *explode*."

"Keep talking," Hugh warned, "and you'll see me explode."

Oh, crap. This scene was not going to end well.

But the door to Fast Shoots opened once more and Devlin was there. She would have been lying to herself if Julianna didn't acknowledge the relief that surged through her.

Devlin's glittering gaze raked from Hugh to John. Tension hardened his jaw. "What the fuck is this?"

"*This,*" Julianna said clearly, "is me leaving." She had to get away from that scene. She didn't know who to trust—John and Hugh? Hell, no. Devlin? Herself?

She turned from them and hurried toward the street. She had to clear her head.

"Julianna!" Devlin called after her.

She didn't stop. Her steps became even faster. The light up ahead was green for pedestrians, so she hurried out and—

"*Julianna!*" That wasn't just her name—it was a roar of fear and fury. Her head snapped to the right, and she saw a black van barreling toward her. The driver wasn't slowing at all—just coming straight for her.

She turned and tried to run back toward the safety of the sidewalk. Everything seemed to be moving in super slow speed around her. Everything but that black van. Closer, closer—

Devlin grabbed her left wrist and he yanked her toward him. He pulled her against his body and they fell back, slamming down toward the sidewalk even as the van hurtled past them. She could smell the exhaust from the van, could nearly feel the rough touch of the vehicle as it lurched past her...

But the van didn't hit her.

They'd made it out of the way.

She pushed up and stared at Devlin. His eyes were open—blazing with emotion—as he said, "Too damn close."

Yes, it had been.

His hand slipped beneath her hair and he pulled her toward him. "Too close," he said again and he kissed her. Deep, hard, desperately.

The same way she was kissing him.

"Uh, yeah…" Lex's voice drifted to them. "I'm glad as all hell that you two are okay, but could you let her go, Dev, long enough for us to get the hell away from the road in case that bastard comes back?"

Julianna lifted her head. Her left hand was still in Devlin's grasp. "Thank you," she told him. He'd saved her, again.

Very carefully, he lifted her up. They rose and turned to stare at the crowd that had gathered around them.

"Tell me," Devlin muttered, "that someone got that joker's tag number."

More whispers from the crowd.

"I got it," John said as he stepped forward.

Her gaze cut to him.

Hugh stood behind the reporter, glowering.

Heather was in jail, Hugh and John were both right there…so who the hell was after her? Who'd just tried to run her down?

Devlin's hands were around her waist. The hands that had pounded into Hugh were trembling against her.

"I got it," John said again, his voice rising even more. "We can get the guy! We can stop him! This is front page news. Front freaking page!"

Lex slapped a hand on Devlin's shoulder. "You just scared the hell out of me."

"Like I was going to let her get hurt."

Julianna glared at him. "What if you'd been hurt right then? You have to think of yourself, too—"

"I'm your bodyguard!" Devlin blasted back. "It's my job to take care of you!"

"You're more than that!' Julianna shouted at him, pushed too far. Then she realized just what she'd said. "You're more than that," she whispered as the words sank in for them both.

"Okay…" Lex drew out the word. "We've got a crowd, and, more importantly, we've got a tag number. *I* saw it, too. So let's call the cops and end this thing."

Julianna couldn't look away from Devlin, but she nodded. Yes, yes, they'd end this. *Now*.

***

Ethan Barclay.
The man was a constant pain in Devlin's ass.

"Did you hear me, Devlin?" Faith demanded. "I told you, that tag belongs to Ethan Barclay. Or, actually, it belongs to his business. So the person who tried to run down your client...that would be the man who pops up way too much at my police precinct."

Ethan wouldn't hurt Julianna. Just like he wouldn't hurt Sophie.

"What's the connection between them?" Faith wanted to know. "I mean, how the hell does he fit into this one?"

Oh, it's just a little matter of murder and cover-up. Blackmail. The usual. "I don't know," he said instead.

She whistled. "I sure hope you're not lying to me."

It wasn't something he wanted to do.

"I've got an APB out for Ethan right now. Seems the guy has gone to ground." She turned away from him and paced toward her desk. "Not like it's the first time he's wanted to dodge the law. Let's just hope that he doesn't decide to flee the country or some crap like that."

Julianna stood a few feet away. There was no emotion on her face, but her eyes were sure dark and stormy. He knew exactly what she was going to say even before he closed in on her and she whispered—

"He *wouldn't*."

He put a finger on her lips. "The cops are handling this, baby. Let's go back to my place."

The storm in her eyes got even worse. The woman really needed to get a bit better at picking up on the silent messages he was sending her — because she seemed to be completely missing what he was telling her.

Julianna whirled away and marched for the police station's door. He was aware of the eyes on them, and he just wanted to get her out—

"You're wrong about Ethan," she called back to Faith.

Oh, hell. *Now* Faith would realize there was definitely a connection between Julianna and the too-notorious Ethan. Devlin peered over his shoulder at the detective.

"I've heard other women say the same thing." Faith tapped her chin. "What is it about that man? I personally like men who are a bit more law abiding…and far less likely to kill an enemy on sight."

Before Julianna could say anything more, Devlin grabbed her elbow and steered her to the door.

"Devlin, stop," she snapped out. "We can't let her think Ethan did this, we can't—"

They were outside. Finally. "Someone else wants us to think he did it."

She frowned. "He *didn't*."

"I don't think so, either." But anyone would be able to peg him as the perfect fall guy. With Ethan's past, the police would jump to arrest him. They certainly had before. "What we need to figure out is this…who knows about your connection to Ethan? Who would know that they could incriminate him with a tie to you?"

A furrow appeared between her brows. "Sophie. She knows. And my sister."

A sister who'd just arrived in town.

"You know," she added. "Your guys at VJS know."

Speaking of VJS…he saw Lex heading toward them. He'd have to get the guy to call Sophie, pronto. Sophie and Ethan shared a pretty powerful past, too—a past that had made Lex jealous on too many occasions. But if anyone could find Ethan right then, Devlin knew it would be Sophie.

"Who else?" Devlin pushed.

"Jeremy knew," she said, biting her lip. "Because of the video, he had to know. He had that security consultant dig it up, right?"

But the consultant was dead.

Maybe someone else close to Jeremy had known, too. Like a step-daughter. Or maybe…

"And…" Julianna rubbed her forehead. "That reporter—John Reynolds. He told me that he'd been talking to Carly. Maybe…it could be possible that she told him."

But John had been at the scene of the near hit-and-run.

"What's happening?" Lex demanded.

"We have to find Ethan Barclay," Devlin said, his voice hard. "Now."

"Fuck," Lex shook his head. "What has he done this time?"

CHAPTER SIXTEEN

Carly heard a faint knock at her door. Frowning, she edged closer to the door. The nice man from VJS — Chance Valentine — had gotten her the apartment. He'd said it was a safe location. He'd also told her that he'd be bringing Julianna by soon so that she could talk with her step-sister.

Is that Julianna now? She put her eye to the peep-hole. A blonde woman was on the other side, her head turned away from Carly. Smiling, Carly opened the door.

The blonde turned toward her.

Not Julianna.

"Hello, there," the blonde said as she lifted her gun and pointed it at Carly. "So glad you came to town." There was something on the end of that gun — the barrel was too long.

A silencer. Dear God, that woman has a silencer on the gun!

"Who are you?"

"I'm the woman who's going to kill you." She was a killer in a perfectly styled suit.

Carly tried to shove that door shut.

But there was a strange whistle of sound. A thud.

The thud was her body hitting the ground. Because she'd been shot. The bullet had torn into her, moving so fast, and just giving a whistle. No bang. No thunder. Such a soft sound. *Because she had a silencer on the gun.*

The blonde headed into the apartment. She grabbed Carly's hands and dragged her away from the door. "Don't die just yet," she said, giving Carly a kick. "I need you to call your dear sister for me. Tell her to get her ass over here, *now.*"

Carly shook her head. "You—"

The tip of the silencer pressed to her head. "I said *now*. So tell me…where the fuck is your phone?"

***

Julianna's phone rang just as they were hurrying away from the police station. She yanked it out and when she saw Carly's name on the screen, she answered immediately. "Carly? What's happening?"

There was a ragged breath. "Julie…I'm…sorry." Carly's voice was weak. "So…sorry."

She stared up at Devlin. *Something is wrong.*
Julianna mouthed those words to him. "Where
are you, Carly?" Devlin had promised that VJS
would take care of her —

"*Don't.*" Carly's voice had grown sharper.
"*Don't come…here.*"

Her heart pounded ever faster. "Carly?"

"Bitch…has a gun…"

Julianna's skin iced.

"Blonde…thought she was you — *ah!*"

Carly's voice ended in a pain-filled cry. The
line went dead.

The phone almost slipped from Julianna's
nerveless fingers. "Where did the VJS put Carly?"
She demanded of Lex and Devlin.

They didn't answer fast enough.

"Where is my sister?"

***

Carly grabbed her stomach. She'd been
shot…*again*. The blood was pumping out of her,
the pain was burning like a knife inside of her,
but she didn't care.

Julianna would be safe.

She hadn't led her sister into a trap. She'd
protected her.

"Julie…won't…" Carly whispered up at the
woman. "Suffer…for me…" Not ever again. Not
ever.

She was dying. She'd take all of the secrets to the grave with her.

"Dumb bitch," her killer muttered.

Carly smiled. She knew these were her last moments. She thought of her sister. Of their bond, a bond that even time hadn't been able to break. And she thought…

Of the man that she'd loved. Wildly, completely. Loved and lost.

If only…

Ethan was on her mind even as her eyelids sagged shut.

***

It was supposed to be a safe house. Sonofabitch…*Julianna's sister should have been safe!* Devlin slammed his car door and raced around, but Julianna had already jumped from the SUV. She was trying to run to the building, but he locked his arms around her stomach and hauled her back. "The perp is up there!" He told her, holding her tight, hating that he had to use his strength to trap her. "You go running in, and you're dead, too."

But Julianna kept fighting him. "Stop it!" She twisted against him. "Let me go, let—"

"*Let her the fuck go,*" Ethan Barclay said as he raced up the sidewalk.

Lex jumped from his car then and ran to intercept the guy.

Ethan threw a punch at Lex when the guy grabbed him. Lex punched back, and they both wound up on the ground.

"Stop it!" Julianna shouted.

The men froze.

"Violence...so sick of the violence!"

Remorse flashed on Ethan's face. "Jules..."

She flinched in Devlin's arms. She wasn't fighting Devlin, and that should have warned him. But he wasn't prepared when she said, "Go, Ethan. Upstairs. Third floor, room 302. Someone hurt Carly."

Something happened to Ethan's face then. Fury rippled in his eyes, and his features twisted with a rage that Devlin had never seen. Ethan leapt away from Lex and ran for the building.

Devlin knew, with utter certainty, that if Ethan found Carly dead upstairs, he'd kill whoever else was in that room.

"Go after him," Julianna said. "We have to!"

Shit, yes, they did. So they ran—him, Julianna, and Lex. Ethan was racing up the stairs and they hurried behind him. When they reached the third floor, Devlin only had a moment to see that the door to room 302 was open.

Then Ethan ran inside. *"No!"* A bellow of rage and fear and pain.

Her sister is dead.

"Julianna," Devlin whispered, hating for her to see what was going to be in that room.

But she ran in. And when he followed, he saw Ethan on his knees beside Carly's still body. His hands were shaking as Ethan reached out to touch her blood-covered stomach. Carly was too pale, the blood too dark on her clothes.

"Jules…" Ethan turned toward Julianna. Tears were in his eyes. "Help me, Jules!"

Julianna fell to the floor beside him. She touched Carly's throat. "She's still alive!" Her frantic gaze met Ethan's. "Call an ambulance!" Then Julianna put her hands on her sister's wounds. "We have to stop the blood flow. That's what they do in the movies. Just put pressure on—"

Ethan's hands covered hers. Devlin yanked out his phone and called for help. He saw the blood soak through their fingers. Julianna and Ethan had their heads pressed close together. They were staring down at Carly, and, as he stared at them, there was no missing their desperation.

Carly mattered, to them both.

Had the killer known that? Is that why she was chosen?

"A blonde," Lex murmured as he came forward from the back of the apartment. Devlin knew he'd been securing the scene. "That's what Carly said, right?"

Yes, but only Carly could identify her attacker. And Carly was barely hanging on for her life.

***

"I traced her phone," Ethan muttered as the EMTs loaded Carly into the ambulance. "How fucking sick and twisted is that? I used my connections and I traced her phone to this place because I needed to see her. I *had* to see her."

His fingers were covered in blood. His gaze was on Carly—and Julianna.

Devlin found that his own gaze was straying back to Julianna, again and again. He hated the fear that cloaked her. The pain.

"You know what it's like," Ethan's voice was haunted as he whispered, "when you're so consumed by a woman…you don't want to imagine a world without her."

Julianna turned toward Devlin.

"I lived without her for too long," Ethan rasped. "Don't make my mistakes. Don't fucking let her go." Then he was brushing by Devlin. He bent, whispered something to Julianna, and she nodded. A few seconds later, Ethan leapt into the back of the ambulance. One of the EMTs tried to push him out, but Ethan just pushed right back.

When the ambulance roared away, Ethan was riding in the back with Carly.

Julianna walked toward Devlin. Beautiful, but too pale. Dark shadows were under her eyes. Her cast seemed to weigh down her arm and he just wanted to wrap her in his arms and protect her.

I want her safe.

"I know who did it," Julianna said simply.

"What? Baby, how the hell do you know that?"

Her gaze cut to the ambulance. "Ethan just told me there was more on that flash drive. We never looked past our video, but he did, just a few hours ago."

And that would explain why the Smith estate had been trashed. Someone else had been looking for the flash drive. Julianna had walked in during the middle of that search, and she'd been attacked.

"I wasn't the only woman Jeremy was blackmailing." Her smile was cold. "Help me to stop her?"

He knew that he would do anything for Julianna. Devlin nodded.

***

Smith Industries had closed for the day. Or, at least, the place *should* have been closed. But when Julianna and Devlin walked inside, they could hear the distinct whir of machines.

Not just any machine…a shredder.

Julianna strode to Jeremy's old office. It had been so long since she'd been there. It was like visiting a grave.

And finding the grim reaper waiting.

A blonde woman was feeding papers into that shredder, as fast as she could. A gun was on the desk beside her.

"Hello, Avery," Julianna said quietly.

Avery Glenn whirled around. She reached out for her gun.

"Don't," Devlin warned her. He had his own weapon out and already trained on Avery.

Avery's pretty face twisted with fury. "You —"

"He was blackmailing you, too, wasn't he?" That was what Ethan had told her...that Jeremy's assistant, Avery Glenn, had been on that damn flash drive too. A video of her and a lover. "I mean, I knew you were his lover, and I frankly didn't care. As long as Jeremy was with you, then he left me the hell alone." Brutal words. "But I didn't know he was blackmailing you, too, not until today. I mean, you gave me that BS line about loving him, but it was just to throw me off, wasn't it?"

Avery just glared at her.

"You tried to kill my sister," Julianna said. "That means...*you're done.*"

But Avery's lips twisted in a taunting smile. "I'm not even close to being done. That would be your dear sister. She's the one with bullets in her. Maybe she should have just followed orders. All she had to do was say for you to come by…for a nice, friendly little visit. Just come by…"

"The police are coming," Julianna told her softly. "We called them on our way over here. You remember Detective Faith Chestang? She'll be here soon. She'll make sure that you're locked up." Julianna considered that for a moment. "She's very good at her job," she added, aware that her voice came out too wooden. Her emotions were all wrapped up, far too tightly, inside of her. If she let her control slip, even for a moment, Julianna feared that *she'd* be the one killing.

Avery laughed. "Why arrest me? There's no evidence…*none.*"

"Carly will testify—"

"Carly's going to die on the operating room table, if she's not dead already." Avery inched a bit closer to the gun. "And it's not like anyone will believe you—you're the woman who killed her husband. Stabbed the bastard thirteen times! No one will believe you…" She gestured to Devlin. "Or the new lover that you have."

Julianna cocked her head to the side. "There's the flash drive." Actually, she wasn't sure it still existed. Maybe Ethan had already destroyed it, but Avery wouldn't know that. "It will provide plenty of evidence."

Avery blanched but quickly recovered. "You don't want that getting out, no more than I do. You want your dirty secrets buried…"

Julianna had put all of the missing pieces together. "You wanted the flash drive very badly, didn't you? *That's* why you were at the house that day. And that's why you sent your partner back the other night. You even gave him a key, didn't you? A key *and* the alarm code so he could get inside and search for those files."

Avery's eyes glittered with her rage. "Where are the files?"

Long gone.

"What did you do?" Devlin asked Avery. "How'd you wind up on his blackmail list?" He moved closer to Avery and he pulled a pair of handcuffs out of his jacket. He'd had the handcuffs—and the gun—secured in his car. Apparently, the agents at VJS believed in being prepared. Julianna was very grateful for that fact.

"*Everyone* was on his list," Avery retorted, apparently feeling that there was nothing left to hide. "He had to control *everyone!* So he found out that I…I was sleeping with a friend's lover. He said he'd tell her. That he'd ruin everything! Like he even knew what my big plan was…"

A friend's lover? Why the hell would that matter to Jeremy? That hardly seemed…

Avery's gaze shifted behind Julianna. The other woman smiled.

Oh, hell.

"I've got a gun pointed at the back of your head," Hugh Bounty announced, his voice carrying and easily recognizable. "And my finger is just itching to pull the trigger."

Devlin's head whipped around, and, in the same instant, he lifted his gun and pointed it at Avery's head. "And I've got a gun pointed at *your* lover's head," he snarled right back. "Do *anything* to hurt Julianna, and you and Avery are both dead."

Silence. That really thick, scary kind.

"Guess that means we're at a stand-off," Hugh said, smiling. "Or maybe…" Now he lunged forward and locked his arm around Julianna's throat. "Maybe I don't give a shit about what happens to Avery at this point. See…she wasn't supposed to sleep with Jeremy fucking Smith. That wasn't part of the plan. But I know what she did…*I know.* "

"*Hugh!*" Avery cried, her mouth dropping open in horror. "What? *No!* I can explain! I did it for us! Just like you did — like you did with Heather!"

They were a damn twisted pair.

And as she felt Hugh's arm lock even tighter around her neck, as she felt the rough strength in the body against hers, Julianna knew he was the man who'd attacked her the other night. He'd been in her house, searching for the files that Avery kept rambling about.

"The money is in my account," Hugh said as he put the gun barrel to Julianna's temple. "You transferred it."

"*Our* account," Avery blasted back at him. "Ours! We're supposed to leave together, we're supposed to—"

"Yeah, about that…" And the gun moved away from Julianna's head. It pointed toward Devlin and Avery. "We're done." He fired.

"*No!*" Julianna screamed. But before the bullet could hit, Devlin grabbed Avery. Their bodies twisted as they fell, and the bullet thudded into the wall, barely missing them.

And while they were fighting to live, Hugh jerked Julianna back. He pulled her hard, yanking her toward the door. "I don't give a fuck about Avery," he yelled at Devlin. "But I know you won't even think of shooting at me while Julianna's near, you won't think—"

A woman's low, ice-cold voice called out, "*He won't, but I will.*"

Julianna's breath sawed out. "We—we didn't come here alone."

Devlin had cuffed Avery. She was on the floor now, sobbing.

"I told you…" Julianna managed. "We didn't come alone."

Devlin lifted his gun and aimed it toward Julianna and Hugh. "I believe you already know Detective Faith Chestang."

Hugh pulled Julianna even closer. His hard grip on her throat was making it difficult to breathe. "A cop won't shoot and risk a civilian's life!"

"She's not a civilian, though," Faith said, her voice still icy, "she's a criminal, just like you. She killed her husband."

His grip tightened again, and she couldn't breathe at all. Julianna clawed at his hands.

"*Let her go!*" Devlin bellowed. "Now!"

"If a killer gets injured," Faith said, her cool voice a sharp contrast to Devlin's roar, "that's something that just can't be—"

"She didn't do it!" Hugh shouted. His hold eased, just enough for Julianna to suck in a desperate breath. "She stabbed the bastard—twice, but then she went down. Avery and I were already planning to kill him that night. We couldn't let him ruin our plans. And when we walked in and the guy was bleeding every fucking where, we knew it was our perfect chance."

Julianna stopped clawing at him as shock settled over her. She…hadn't killed Jeremy?

"He was already weak from blood loss. I held him down, and Avery drove the knife into him."

Avery lunged forward. "*Shut up!*"

Devlin grabbed her and pushed her back down. "You two…you were running a con. One that involved the step-daughter."

Hugh laughed. "Not just a con, buddy. *The* con. I got close to Heather. Avery got in good with the boss man. *Only she wasn't supposed to fuck him!* We learned all his secrets, learned just how *he* was skimming and cheating the company, then we took that money. We funneled it into our own account."

But something had gone wrong. "He found out," Julianna managed to gasp out, "that you and Avery were sleeping together. He…"

"He said he was going to tell Heather," Hugh finished, speaking fast and wildly now. "The transfer wasn't finished. We couldn't risk everything blowing up on us — we had to stop the bastard! And then we thought that maybe he knew what we were really doing…that he was coming for us." He backed up a few more steps, dragging Julianna with him once more. "It's the law of the business world, right?" He grunted. "Kill or fucking *be* killed."

"No," Faith said softly. "That's not the business world."

Hugh shoved the gun barrel deeper into Julianna's temple. "You can't kill an innocent victim. You *won't* shoot her. And the bodyguard over there…he's so in love with her that he can't stand the idea of hurting her. Can't even let her get a damn bruise without him flipping out!"

So in love with her.

No, that was wrong. Devlin wanted her, but he didn't love her.

He didn't.

But…

Julianna looked at him. Devlin was lowering his weapon. "Don't shoot, Faith," Devlin ordered. "Offer the bastard some kind of deal, but *don't shoot.*"

"See what I mean?" Hugh's breath blew over Julianna's ear. "He knows that if anyone fires at me, my finger will be squeezing this trigger, and you'll be dead. He can't let that happen. He needs you too much."

No, I need him. "Do you love me?" Julianna asked Devlin. She wanted to know, before the next moments passed. Before there was no turning back. No time to think of what could have been.

He put the gun down on the desk. "Yes."

That was nice. That was…good. "Thank you."

"Julianna—"

She lifted her right wrist, swinging fast with that cast, and she slammed it back into Hugh's face. She prepared herself for the blast of gunfire, sure that he'd fire but not willing to take the chance that he'd turn that weapon on Devlin again. But there wasn't a blast. Hugh swore and his fingers clawed at her throat as he staggered back. So she hit him again with her cast. Harder. She felt something smash—maybe the cast, maybe a bone—she didn't really care. She hit him again—

Devlin's arms wrapped around her and he pulled her back, pushing her behind his body even as he drove his fist toward Hugh.

She didn't flinch away from the violence. She did grab the gun Devlin had left on the desk. She lifted it up, aimed it—

"Freeze," Faith said. She had her gun inches away from Hugh's face.

And Julianna had hers aimed at Hugh's heart.

Hugh froze.

Julianna's fingers trembled on the gun. Hugh and Avery—a sobbing Avery who was now huddled on the floor near the desk—they'd tried to destroy her life. They'd nearly killed Carly. They'd attacked Julianna again and again. She'd been charged with *murder* while they stood back and waited for her to spend the rest of her life in jail.

In that moment, she wanted to pull the trigger more than she wanted anything else.

"Baby." Devlin stepped in front of her gun. "Baby, you're going to be free now."

"Carly…" Julianna whispered.

"She's a fighter, just like you. She's going to make it."

He couldn't know that.

"I know what you want to do. You think I don't want to take out that bastard, too?" He wrapped his fingers around the gun. "But you can't do that. Not you." His voice dropped and he softly promised, "I'll do it for you."

What? She sucked in a sharp breath. "No, Dev—"

"You think I won't? He tried to kill you. He *hurt* you. I will make him suffer. I will make him pay. I will—"

She yanked the gun back and dropped it on the desk. Then she was grabbing Devlin and holding him tight. "No, not you! That's not you!" Devlin was good. Devlin was strong. Devlin was *hers.* "I love you," she told him, frantic. "I need you. I need you with me. *Don't*…Just…be with me." *Don't shoot him. Don't go to jail for me. Don't suffer for me.*

She kissed him. Desperate, near breaking.

Be with me.

Stay…always, with me.

She could taste her own tears in that kiss.

There were other voices then. The thunder of more footsteps. When Julianna slowly pulled away from Devlin and opened her eyes, she saw a line of cops filling the office. Hugh was cuffed and on his knees. Avery was talking fast, shouting, "It was all Hugh! He did it all!"

"Right," Faith drawled, sounding highly doubtful. "I'm sure you'll tell me all about it at the station. Though you might want to think about getting a lawyer…"

"But—"

"You have the right to remain silent," Faith began.

Devlin's fingers curled under her chin, and he slowly turned Julianna's head back toward him. "How about we get the hell out of here?"

There would be questions. Dozens of them from the cops. She'd have to do interviews, interrogations. Things weren't over. Not yet.

But…

I'm not scared anymore. The fear was finally gone. Julianna stared up at him. "Where are we going to go?"

"Any damn place you want," he promised her. "*Any place.*" Then he kissed her again.

She didn't feel the throbbing in her wrist. Didn't hear the rumble of voices anymore. Didn't worry about the specter of her past and the ghost of her dead husband.

She only felt Devlin. His touch. His kiss.

His strength. A strength that would never hurt her. Only protect her.

He loved her.

And she…she would do anything for him.
Even give up vengeance.

And start dreaming of a future once again.

EPILOGUE

Devlin hurried down the hospital corridor, two hot cups of coffee cradled in his hands. Julianna had been sitting at her sister's bedside for hours, and he wanted to get back to her. Carly was going to pull through, he was sure of it, and then they could all start healing together.

A nearby elevator dinged and the doors opened. He walked past that elevator and—

"Devlin."

He glanced back. Faith Chestang had just stepped from the elevator. Her badge gleamed from its position on her hip.

"I came here to find you," she said, heading toward him. "You and Julianna."

"Julianna's in her sister's room." Just seeing the detective put him on alert. He didn't want anyone coming after Julianna—or Carly.

"There are a few things I think you both should know…"

Hell. "Do we need a lawyer?" Devlin asked bluntly.

She smiled. "Not this time. I've got the killers, and they aren't getting away."

They'd better not.

"Those mysterious files that they kept talking about…Ethan Barclay confessed to me that he destroyed the files. He said he didn't realize what they were, but I'm guessing they held some blackmail info on him. He didn't want anyone accessing that material, so he made sure the flash drive was no doubt obliterated."

"No doubt," Devlin murmured.

"I don't quite understand the connection between Julianna and Ethan…"

He didn't speak.

"But judging by the way he went batshit when she was brought to the hospital, I'd say the connection has to be tied to Julianna's sister, Carly."

Devlin shrugged. "The coffee's hot. If you want to come in and talk with us both—"

"Would you have killed him?" Faith asked.

He'd wondered when she would ask him that.

"Because I heard what you said to Julianna. She wanted to shoot Hugh. Can't say that I blame her, but you—you offered to do it. Offered to do the crime and the time, all for her."

He smiled at her. "Maybe I was just trying to get her to drop the gun," he murmured. "Maybe I knew just what she'd do."

Faith's head cocked as she studied him. "And how the hell would you know that? *I* wasn't even sure what she'd do, and I've seen plenty of perps and victims in my time. That woman was at the edge. For a minute there, I was even afraid she might shoot you."

He'd never been afraid of that. "I trusted her."

"You probably shouldn't have," she muttered.

His smile grew. "You ever been in love, Faith?" It was a trick question. He knew all about Faith's secret affair with one of the most powerful men in D.C.

She just stared at him.

"Think about what you'd do to protect the person you love. You believe I was bluffing? That I was just telling Julianna all that to get her to drop the gun?" He laughed. "I love her. And I would do *anything* for her." He turned away and headed down the hall.

"Even kill?" She called after him. "Because that is some twisted shit."

Maybe he was twisted. Maybe he was damaged inside. Maybe he had more of his parents in him than he wanted to admit.

But the truth was…when it came to Julianna, there wasn't anything he wouldn't do. If she'd told him to shoot Hugh Bounty…

That guy would have been in a body bag.

He turned the corner of that hospital corridor and saw Julianna. She saw him and a wide grin swept across her face. "Carly's awake!" A bright smile lit her face and tears glinted in her eyes. "She's going to make it!" She threw her arms around him and held tight.

Devlin kept a careful grip on the coffee, not letting so much as a drop spill on her.

After all, Julianna was what mattered to him.

And protecting her…loving her…that was the job he wanted for the rest of his life.

Turn the page for a sneak peek at Cynthia Eden's brand new dark & sexy romantic suspense series from Avon Romance…

BOOK 1: BROKEN

The first novel in *New York Times* bestselling author Cynthia Eden's sizzling LOST series introduces the Last Option Search Team, an elite unit that must protect the only surviving victim of a serial killer.

Ex-SEAL and LOST founder Gabe Spencer is accustomed to the unusual in his job. But when knockout Eve Gray steps into his office, he's rattled. For the mysterious woman is a dead ringer for the heiress thought to be the latest prey of the serial killer who goes by the name Lady Killer.

When Eve awoke in an Atlanta hospital, her past was a blank slate. Then she recognized her own face in the newspaper and vowed to learn the truth. Determined to confront the nightmares hidden in her mind, she never expects to find a partner in Gabe.

As Gabe and Eve work together, their explosive attraction becomes irresistible. Gabe knows that his desire for Eve is growing too strong, bordering on a dangerous obsession, but nothing pulls him away from her. And when another Eve lookalike disappears, Gabe vows to protect Eve at all costs. While Eve may have forgotten the killer in her past, it's clear he hasn't forgotten *her*.

Keeping reading for a special look at the prologue and the first chapter from BROKEN…

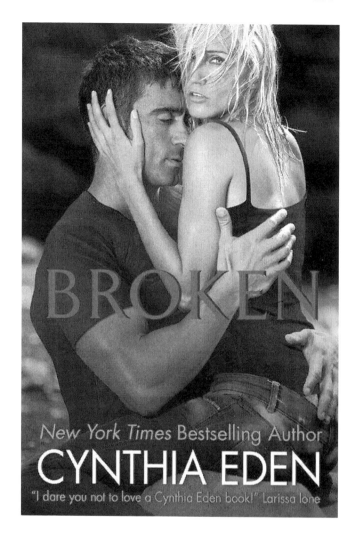

New York Times Bestselling Author

CYNTHIA EDEN

"I dare you not to love a Cynthia Eden book!" Larissa Ione

BROKEN. Copyright © 2015 by Cindy Roussos. All rights reserved. Printed in the United States of America. No part of this book may be used or reproduced in any manner whatsoever without written permission except in the case of brief quotations embodied in critical articles and reviews. For information address HarperCollins Publishers, 195 Broadway, New York, NY 10007.

HarperCollins books may be purchased for educational, business, or sales promotional use. For information please write: Special Markets Department, HarperCollins Publishers, 195 Broadway, New York, NY 10007.

ISBN 9780062349569

PROLOGUE - BROKEN

She could smell the ocean and hear the pounding of the surf. She could see the sky above her, so very blue and clear, but she couldn't move at all.

Her body had gone numb hours ago. At first the numbness had been a blessing. She'd just wanted the pain to stop, and it had. She didn't even scream any longer. What would be the point? There was no one around to hear her. No one was coming to help her.

Seagulls cried out, circling above her. She didn't want them to fly down. What if they started to peck at her? *Please, leave me alone.*

Her mouth was dry, filled with bits of sand. Tears had dried on her cheeks.

"Why are you still alive?" The curious voice came from beside her because he was there, watching, as he'd watched for hours. "Why don't you give in? You know you want to just close your eyes and let go."

She did. She wanted to close her eyes and pretend that she was just having a bad dream. A nightmare. When her eyes opened again, she'd be someplace different. Someplace without monsters.

He came closer to her, and she felt something sharp slide into the sand with her. A knife. He liked to use his knife. It pricked her skin, but then he lifted the knife and pressed the blade against her throat.

"I can end this for you. Do it now. Just tell me …" His words were dark. Tempting. "Tell me that you want to die."

The surf was so close. She'd always loved the ocean. But she'd never expected to die like this. She didn't *want* to die like this. She realized the tears weren't dry on her face.

She was still crying. Her cheeks were wet with tears and blood.

"Tell me," he demanded. *"Tell me that you want to die."*

She shook her head. Because death wasn't what she wanted. Even after all he'd done, she didn't want to stop living.

She didn't want to give up.

The knife sliced against her neck. A hoarse moan came from her lips. Her voice had broken when she screamed and screamed. She should have known better than to scream.

That was what he'd told her. *You should know better, sweetheart. It's just you and me. Until your last breath.*

Her blood mixed with the sand. He was angry again. Or … no, he'd always been angry. She just hadn't seen the rage, not until it was too late. Now she couldn't look at him at all. No matter what he did to her, she *wouldn't* look at him.

She didn't want to remember him this way. Actually, she didn't want to remember him at all.

Her gaze lifted to the blue sky. To those circling seagulls.

I want to fly, Daddy. She'd been six the first time she'd come to the island and seen the gulls. *I want to fly like them.*

Her father had laughed and told her that it looked like she'd lost her wings.

She'd lost more than that.

"I want to fly," she whispered.

"Too bad, because you're not flying anywhere. You're going to die here."

But there was no death for her yet, and she wasn't begging.

The gulls were blurry now, because of her tears.

He'd buried her in the sand, covering her wounds and packing the sand in tightly around her. Only her head and some of her neck remained uncovered. Her hands were bound, or so he thought.

But she'd been working beneath the sand. Working even as the moments ticked so slowly past, and he kept taunting her.

He had taken his time with this little game. Tried to break her in those endless hours.

She wouldn't be broken.

Her hands were free. If he'd just move that knife away from her neck …

He lifted the knife and stabbed it into the sand — into the sand right over her left shoulder. She choked out a cry as the sharp pain pierced her precious numbness.

"You'll beg soon," he told her. Then he was on his feet. Stalking away from her. "They all do."

He'd left the knife in her shoulder and made the mistake of turning his back on her.

She'd lived this long … if she was going out, she'd fight until her last breath.

Her fingers were free. She just had to escape the sand. The heavy sand that he'd packed and packed around her.

Burying me.

She could feel the faint cracks start to slip across the sand as she shifted. Her strength was almost gone, but she could do this. She *had* to do it. If she didn't, she was dead.

He was turning back toward her.

Move! The scream was in her head, and she managed to lunge up. Her right hand grabbed the hilt of the knife. She jerked the blade out of her shoulder and surged to her feet even as the sand rained down her body.

He was yelling, screaming at her. She didn't care. She charged forward and slammed the knife into his chest. Their eyes met. It was the only time she'd looked into his gaze since the torture had begun.

She saw herself reflected in his stare.

He fell, slumping back. She didn't stop to see if he was still alive. She didn't care. She raced for the edge of the beach, for the little boat that was anchored just offshore. Then she was stumbling into the surf. The water was icy against her skin, and she knew her blood was turning the water red.

She wasn't afraid of sharks. Men were the killers. Men just like—

"Don't leave me!" His bellow.

He was still alive. He was coming after her.

She fell into the boat. Fumbled. She'd been around boats her whole life. She could start the motor, even with hands that wouldn't stop trembling. She could start—

The motor growled. She shoved the throttle forward. The boat surged away from that little beach, jumping, bouncing over the waves.

He was still shouting. She was laughing. Crying. Not looking back.

She would never look back. Never. He hadn't broken her. Hadn't killed her.

She gazed up at the gulls. *I want to fly.*

Then the boat hit the rocks. Heavy rocks that she'd known were out there, but she'd tried to maneuver around them too late. The boat twisted and shot into the air.

And, in the next instant, she really was flying. Flying and then slamming face first into the water. The water was so red.

Her blood.

She tried to kick back to the surface. She wouldn't give up.

But her body was so tired. The numbness … it had vanished. Pain was back. A deep agony that cut into every muscle.

The surface was farther away. She could just see the outline of the gulls above her.

I want to fly.

She tried to swim. Tried to reach the surface. She didn't want to die.

But she didn't have the strength to fight anymore. The waves rolled around her, and the seagulls vanished.

CHAPTER ONE - BROKEN

Her stomach twisted as Eve Gray gazed up at the imposing building centered on the busy Atlanta street. Heat rose from the pavement, seeming to surround her. Someone bumped her from behind, and she took a quick step forward.

Just one step, then she caught herself.

Her heart was racing so fast, too fast, and her palms were sweating. She brushed her palms over her narrow skirt, and then Eve took just a moment to smooth down her hair.

This was it. The moment she'd been waiting for. The people inside would either help her or—

No, there is no option. They have to help me.

She straightened her shoulders and headed through the big swinging doors. She kept her gaze focused straight in front of her as she marched toward the elevator. She needed to go up to the fourth floor. Suite 409.

The elevator doors opened silently. Men and women in expensive business clothes climbed on and off the elevator. Eve kept her chin up. Her clothes were older, faded, too casual for this office building, but it wasn't like she had a lot of choice.

There were *no* choices for her.

The elevator dinged, and she hurried out onto the fourth floor. The lush carpet swallowed her footsteps. Then, a few desperate moments later, she was standing in front of a heavy, wooden door. Across the door, golden letters spelled: lost.

Her lips curved in a smile that just felt sad. *Lost.* Yes, that was exactly what she was. And she desperately needed the people inside that office to help her.

Eve turned the doorknob with trembling fingers and crept inside. A perky receptionist glanced up at her, showing a smile that flashed huge dimples. "Welcome to Lost, how may I help you?"

Eve had to swallow twice in order to ease the dryness of her throat. "I need to speak with Gabe Spencer." He was the man she'd read about in the paper. The tough ex-SEAL who'd made it his new mission to create LOST.

LOST … the Last Option Search Team. This office and all of the personnel in it had one function, just one—to find missing people. To search for those that the authorities had already given up on.

The receptionist, a pretty girl with sun-streaked blond hair, gave a small shake of her head. "I'm sorry but do you have an appointment, ma'am?"

"No." And Eve knew that the perky lady was about to tell her to hit the road. So Eve shoved her hands into her oversize bag—the only bag that she had—and yanked out a carefully folded newspaper. She smoothed out the folds and offered the paper to the receptionist. "I need to talk with Mr. Spencer about this." *This* being the series of murders that had been highlighted in the *Atlanta News* three weeks ago. Seven women had been abducted. Tortured. Killed.

Their murderer hadn't been caught.

"We don't … um … we don't really hunt serial killers here at LOST," the receptionist said with wide eyes. "I'm not sure what you think Mr. Spencer can do for you—"

The office door opened behind the receptionist. At the soft sound, Eve glanced up automatically and saw a man—tall, handsome, powerful—filling that doorway. His hair was jet-black, thick, and still military short, even though she knew the guy wasn't active with the SEALs any longer.

Gabe Spencer.

She'd done research on him at the local library. Found his picture. Read his bio, again and again. Thirty-four. Single. Master's degree in criminal justice. He'd been a decorated SEAL, but he'd left the Navy after his sister had been abducted a few years ago. Gabe had made it his sole mission to find Amy and bring her home.

He had brought her home, just not alive.

His gaze was a bright, intense blue, and that gaze focused sharply on Eve. She shifted beneath his stare as uncertainty twisted within her.

He was handsome. No, almost *too* perfect. But his features had looked softer in the pictures she'd seen online. In person, his jaw was sharp and square, his cheeks high, his nose a strong blade … and his lips were sensual. The man had a deep, powerful appeal that seemed to fill the air and —

And she was just staring at him. Heat stained her cheeks. *What is wrong with me?*

"I don't think we can help you," the receptionist told Eve, giving a sad shake of her head.

But Eve wasn't really paying attention to the blonde any longer. She was too aware of Gabe.

Gabe was still staring straight at her, too. His gaze dipped from her face down to her toes — the toes that peeked out from her high heels — then it slowly rose to study her face once more. His voice was a deep rumble as he asked, "Have we met, Ms. …?"

She almost laughed at his question. "I'm afraid that I don't know if we have."

One dark brow lifted as confusion flashed in his blue gaze.

"I'm here to meet with you, Mr. Spencer." The words came out in a rush, but this was her chance. She had to take it. Eve grabbed her newspaper back from the receptionist. "Please, can you spare a few minutes to talk with me?"

That bright stare seemed to weigh her. Eve tensed. She was used to people assessing her. It was all they seemed to do lately. Assess. Judge. Find her lacking.

"She doesn't have an appointment," the not-so-perky-now blonde said. "I was just telling her—"

"Melody, I think I can spare a few minutes," he said, and stepped back. Gabe gave a little wave of his hand, indicating the open door. "If you'd like to come inside, we can talk privately."

Eve's knees were trembling as she hurried forward. At least she didn't trip or do anything to embarrass herself. *Yet.* This meeting was important. No, this meeting was *everything.* She had to get Gabe Spencer to help her. If he didn't help her, she had no idea what she'd do next.

The office smelled of leather. A bright expanse of windows looked over downtown Atlanta. Gabe's desk was huge, taking up a third of the room. She sat across from that big desk, sinking into one of the leather chairs. She expected him to assume a position behind his desk. Instead, he strode toward the left side of the desk, the side close to her, and he paused. His arms crossed over his chest as his gaze raked her once more.

"Is someone missing?" His question was low, sympathetic.

Eve gave a small nod, then offered him her newspaper.

Frowning, he read the headline. "The Lady Killer?" Gabe shook his head. "I know they recovered some bodies after the last hurricane swept through that area, but I don't see—"

"They haven't recovered all of the bodies. S-Some are still missing." Her fingers twisted in her lap. According to the newspaper, there were seven suspected abductions and murders. But only four bodies had been found so far.

Three women were still missing.

His gaze scanned over the article. Then, after a few moments, he glanced back up at her. "You want me to find one of the missing women?"

He wasn't getting it. "O-Open the paper."

Frowning, he opened it. Pictures of the missing women were inside. Grainy pictures. Black and whites but …

"I don't need you to find a missing woman."

"That's what we do." His gaze was on the photos, not her. There was a slight southern drawl beneath his words, just a little growl of sound, barely noticeable. "We search for the missing. We—" He broke off and she saw his gaze widen. Slowly, very, very slowly, that bright blue stare came back to her face. This time she felt his stare like a physical touch on her.

Eve licked her lips and said, "I don't need you to find a missing woman ... because I'm pretty sure ... I think—I think I *am* one of the missing. I'm one of the Lady Killer's victims, only I'm not dead like they say in the paper."

Gabe Spencer wasn't talking. So Eve let her words tumble out. She didn't want him to think she was crazy. She needed his help too much. "I'm not dead. I just ... I don't remember anything. I can't remember anything that happened to me before June third of this year."

"And what happened on June third?" he asked, voice lacking all emotion.

"That was the day I woke up in St. Helen's Hospital." She'd woken to a room of white. To the sterile scent of cleaners and disinfectants. To the steady drone of machines.

And it had felt ... *wrong*.

I should have heard the waves. Should have smelled the ocean. Those had been her first thoughts, but after them, she'd remembered nothing of her life. No names. No faces. No memories at all.

He just stared at her.

Her heartbeat thudded in her ears. "I'm not lying." Desperation cracked beneath the words. "You can check at the hospital, and they'll verify everything that I've told you."

Dissociative amnesia. That was what one of the doctors had told her she had. She'd sustained a strong blow to her head. Some memory loss was common after an injury like that.

But she wasn't just talking about *some* memory loss. She'd lost everything.

"I need your help," Eve told him, and she knew it sounded like she was begging—she was. "Because what's missing … my life is missing. *I'm* missing." She stood on trembling legs and went to his desk. She looked down at the paper that had fallen to his desktop. Her fingers touched the picture of the beautiful smiling woman. A woman that *could* be her. "If that's me, then I want to know what happened." She glanced over at him. "I want my life back, Mr. Spencer."

"Call me Gabe."

A hard order as his gaze traveled carefully over her every feature. She couldn't read the expression in his eyes. She wanted to, so badly.

"Have you gone to the police with your story?" he asked.

Her lips tightened. "The abductions and murders happened along the southern Gulf Coast. Not here in Atlanta. They don't see the connection." And she believed the detective that she'd spoken with had just thought she was crazy. Since one of her endless doctors had been giving her a psych evaluation at the time, the cop had probably felt pretty justified in that opinion.

A faint line appeared between Gabe's brows. "No one has escaped from the Lady Killer."

"No one that you know about." Her fingers were shaking when she lifted them up to her neck. She pulled her hair back and pointed to the raised flesh, the long, white scar that slid around the left side of her throat. Usually, her hair covered that scar. She didn't want people staring at it and asking questions she couldn't answer. But this time … the scar could actually help her. Maybe. "I think that I got away from him."

In the next instant, Gabe was in front of her. To be such a big guy, he sure could move quickly. When his warm, strong hands touched her skin, Eve flinched, totally unprepared for the hot surge of awareness that shot through her. For months her body had been poked and prodded by dozens of specialists. She'd felt nothing. Been too numb. But one touch from Gabe …

Her gaze darted to his face. There was no sexual awareness in his gaze. No, his eyes were narrowed and intent on the scar that slid around the left side of her neck. "I—I have more scars," she whispered. She'd been ashamed of them at first, so many injuries, but if they were proof, if they could help her … "Someone used a knife on me." Long, deep slices. Two on her stomach. One on her thigh. One on her back. One on her left shoulder.

His fingers were caressing her neck, lightly stroking her skin.

He was tall, had to be about six-foot-three or six-foot-four, so she had to tilt her head back to fully meet his gaze. "Help me? Please?"

Their faces were so close. If someone came inside that office, they'd probably think they were embracing. *Lovers.* And, for just the briefest of moments, she did see a burning flash of awareness in Gabe's eyes. A surge of heat. Desire.

Her body tensed.

That flash vanished from his gaze. "Let me learn more," he said, voice guarded, "then I'll see about taking the case."

She nodded, refusing to let her hope slip away. But there was just one more thing. Unfortunately. She kept her chin up as she confessed, "I don't have any money. I can't pay you. I mean, if you take—" Her cheeks burned as she tried to press on. "I can work for you. I can help at LOST, I can do anything, just—"

Help me stop being no one.

Gabe seemed to shrug that concern way. "We'll work out payment later. *If* I take your case."

He stepped away from her. She immediately missed the warmth of his body. What was wrong with her? She didn't react this way to men. She didn't react this way to anyone.

"I'll need to see your medical reports. Need to know where you were found before you were brought to the hospital. *Who* brought you in. I'll want to talk to all of your doctors."

Eve nodded quickly. "Right, of course."

A muscle flexed along his hard jaw. "If you're lying to me, you'll come to regret it very quickly."

The words held a silken menace.

"Why would I lie?" Eve whispered. Who would want this life? No, not a life. *Nothing.*

"Because the woman that you claim to be, the woman in that picture … Jessica Montgomery … her family is very, very wealthy."

It wasn't about the money. It was about being *someone.*

"I look just like her." Her words were hoarse. There was no way she and that woman could share the same face. That wasn't a coincidence.

"All of the Lady Killer's victims are similar in appearance. Blond hair, green eyes, mid-twenties." A pause. "Beautiful."

She shifted uncomfortably before him. "If I'm not her, then I'm still someone. My life is missing. Just … I want it back. I want to know what happened to me."

After a long, tense moment, he nodded, but said, "Sometimes, you should be careful what you want in this world. If you are one of the Lady

Killer's victims, what do you think will happen next?"

Goose bumps rose onto her arms.

"From all accounts, he stalked these women. Chose them specifically. They are his targets. His prey. Wonder how he'll react when he realizes that one of his victims got away?"

She could feel all of the blood draining from her head. For just an instant she could smell the scent of the ocean. Could hear the cry of a seagull.

No, that wasn't a seagull. It was a scream. *My scream?*

Her mouth had gone dust dry with fear, but she still managed to say, "I—I want my life back."

"Then let's get started." His head inclined toward her, and Eve wondered if she'd just passed some kind of test. And if he had been deliberately pushing her, she couldn't help but wonder … what would have happened if she'd failed his test?

***

The gorgeous blonde with the bedroom eyes and the never-ending legs lived in a homeless shelter.

Gabe watched her from his position across the street. She didn't realize that he'd followed her from LOST. The woman who'd called herself Eve Gray — but who claimed to be someone else entirely, perhaps Jessica Montgomery — had seemed oblivious to everyone and everything as she made her way back through the busy Atlanta streets.

She hadn't taken a taxi. Hadn't jumped into a waiting car.

She'd cut through the streets. Carefully counted out change for a bus.

And hadn't even noticed him slide onto the same bus with her.

Her head stayed down for most of the trip and she didn't talk to anyone. There were plenty of men who stopped to give her admiring glances. When you looked like her, it would be hard not to attract attention.

Oval face. High cheekbones. Small button of a nose. Lips red and plump. And those eyes … one look, and he'd found himself edging closer to her. Wanting to touch. *Needing* to touch.

That sure as hell wasn't the way he normally acted. His iron-tight control was legendary. He didn't look into a pair of big green eyes and think …

Want.

Not usually. But today he had.

He'd wanted. So he'd brought her into his office, even though he had three other appointments waiting. He'd brought her inside so he could get closer to her. Gabe had inhaled the light, sexy scent of her. Watched as her long legs moved a bit nervously beneath her skirt.

Then he'd heard her story.

He had been enraged when he'd seen the scar on her neck. The rush of rage hadn't been expected. He'd heard some brutal stories during his time at LOST, but his elemental fury at just seeing her scar … *What the hell had been up with that?*

She could be bullshitting him. It wouldn't be the first time someone had come in LOST with a bogus story. There were plenty of people out there willing to lie, steal, or even kill in order to get what they wanted.

And what they wanted? It was usually money.

The kind of money that Jessica Montgomery's family had in freaking spades.

A homeless shelter.

Gabe recognized the building on Lortimer Lane for exactly what it was. He just hadn't expected Eve to stop there, but she was rushing inside as if this were a normal routine for her. As if she belonged there.

Her medical files were on their way to his office. He'd be going to see her doctors soon. But right then …

Gabe found himself walking across the street and following her into the shelter.

He'd just stepped inside the doorway when a big, hulking, giant of a guy shoved one hand against his chest. "Where you think you're goin', buddy?" the man demanded, his voice a rumble that sounded like thunder.

Gabe raised his brows. "I need to talk with Eve." He threw her name out, waiting for a response. If Eve was a regular there, then—

The man's hand slammed harder into his chest. Gabe didn't so much as move as the guy barked, "You stay away from Eve!"

Ah, this hadn't been part of the plan. The man's face was flushed a deep red, his bald head glinting, and it looked for all the world like he was about to start swinging punches.

Gabe figured he could take the guy, but fighting his way inside the shelter hadn't been on the day's agenda.

Guess the agenda just changed.

"Pauley, stop!" Eve's voice. High. Scared. Then she was there, running back toward them with a clatter of her high heels.

That was then he noticed that her heels were old, scuffed. The top and skirt that molded to her body so well—showing off her high, round breasts, and slim hips—the outfit hugged her so tightly because it was the wrong size.

Not her clothes.

Eve put a hand on Pauley's hunched shoulders. "He's a friend, Pauley."

Pauley's gaze darted to her. He shook his head and didn't move his hand from Gabe's chest. "No one … no one's supposed to follow you … Guarding door. I always guard."

"Yes, you do." Now her voice was soothing. She smiled at the man. Pauley looked like he was in his early forties. Tattoos slid down his arms. Dozens of them. Faces. Symbols. "And you guard us all very well. But it's okay for Gabe to be here. He won't hurt me."

The guy hesitated a minute longer, then slowly dropped his hold.

Gabe caught the fast exhalation of breath from Eve. "Thank you, Pauley," she whispered. "I'm so glad you're here to keep us safe."

Pauley shuffled back and resumed what Gabe now realized was his guard position at the door.

Eve bit her lip. She probably didn't mean to look sexy. He shouldn't have found her sexy. But there was something about her …

I followed her. Tracked her down. Not for the case. Because I couldn't let her leave. He'd passed off his appointments to his right-hand man, Wade Monroe, just so he could be free to track Eve.

"We need to talk," Gabe heard himself say.

"I'm assuming so." She offered a faint smile. "Since you followed me." Her cheeks held a pink tint, as if she were embarrassed. "Maybe we could talk outside?"

"Where's your room?" Gabe asked instead, just to see her response.

The pink deepened. "We don't … we don't have rooms here. Just beds." Then her chin lifted. Determined pride was there, in her eyes, in her posture.

Pauley had taken up his position a few feet away. Since the guy was so close, they didn't have much privacy, and Gabe definitely wanted privacy with her. Actually, he wanted her completely alone. "You're staying here?" Just so he was clear.

Eve nodded. "Ever since I got out of the hospital." She eased back and stepped into a small corridor. He followed her. "It's not exactly easy to get work when you don't have a real name, much less a social security number. And no work means …"

No money.

She cleared her throat. "I'm sure you understand."

Yeah, he did. Gabe looked around the old building. In the next room, he could see a row of cots. Not beds. Cots. "You shouldn't be here." For some reason, the fact that she was there … it pissed him off. She didn't belong there.

Where does she belong?

"It's better than being on the street." Her chin was still up. "And you're going to help me now, right? You're going to help me get my life back?

Once I know who I am, then I can get out of here. I can get my name. Get a job. Get a home."

Not a shelter.

His gaze locked with hers. He wanted her out of that place right then.

"You're helping me?" Eve pressed.

Dammit. He hadn't even started the research on her. The woman could be playing him. If she was, she'd regret it. He'd make sure of it. But for that moment ... with Pauley muttering behind them ... with a social worker frowning and heading toward them ... all Gabe could say was, "Yes, I'm helping you." He'd find out all of her secrets. Good, bad, and everything in between. Maybe she'd regret it. Maybe he would. But from this moment on he and Eve would be tied together.

Until the case was closed.

***

Gabe returned to LOST, adrenaline pumping through him. He spared a glance for the receptionist, Melody Gaines. "Call the team into my office."

Eyes wide, she nodded and reached for her phone.

He hurried inside his office, the memory of Eve's intense gaze following him. The memory of *her* following him.

When she didn't have any memories of her own.

He dropped into his chair. Rubbed a hard hand over his face. He'd never taken a case like this before. Normally, his team *found* the missing. They started with a case, found the person ... or sadly and far more often, they found the person's body. The remains.

This time, they were starting *with* the body. A very live one.

A faint knock sounded at his door, then the heavy wood opened and Victoria Palmer poked her head inside. A small pair of glasses perched on her nose, and she had her long dark hair pulled back at the nape of her neck. "We've got a new case?" Excitement hummed in her voice.

He nodded.

She rushed inside. "Do I have to wait on the others, or can you spill now?" Nervous energy seemed to bubble just beneath her surface. That was the way she always appeared. Tense, moving, on the verge of ... something.

"You don't have to wait long," a low voice drawled from the doorway. "We're here." And Wade Monroe strode inside. Not an excess of energy from him. Slow, deliberate steps.

Dean Bannon followed right on his heels. Dean's assessing gaze landed on Gabe. "I'm guessing this has to do with the pretty blonde?"

"What blonde?" Victoria demanded. "I didn't see—"

"Sarah's out on another case today," Gabe said, referring to the psychiatrist he kept on staff at LOST. "So go ahead and shut the door. I'll brief her later."

Dean shut the door. Gabe's team—his *top* team—because there were dozens of other support personnel who worked for LOST, closed in. They took the chairs around his desk and waited for their intel.

Gabe's gaze swept over them. Each team member had been chosen because of the specific skills he or she possessed. When Gabe had started LOST, he'd wanted the best personnel working for him. He knew that his team was truly the last chance for many families. Those families *deserved* the best.

So he'd stolen Dr. Victoria Palmer away from Stanford. The forensic anthropologist was using her talents in the field now, and not just in the lecture hall. As for Wade Monroe, the decorated ex-Atlanta detective could dig to the truth faster than anyone Gabe had ever seen. Wade didn't mind getting his hands dirty. In fact, the guy seemed to relish that part of the business. Wade wasn't afraid of danger. He thrived on it. And his personal loss had made him a prime candidate for a position at LOST.

"You're keeping us in suspense," Dean murmured, his voice calm and flat. Totally without emotion or accent.

Dean had been working with the FBI when Gabe approached him. An agent in the Violent Crimes Division, Dean had known all about the real monsters who hunted in the world. And he knew how to *hunt* those monsters. With LOST, Dean had the chance to do plenty of hunting, without so much red tape holding him back.

As for the missing team member … Sarah Jacobs … Sarah was just as vital to the LOST unit. She had a fistful of degrees, but it was her experience as a psychiatrist and a profiler that mattered most to Gabe. When they tracked the missing, Sarah created victim profiles and profiles for their abductors. Their killers. Dean hunted the monsters, but it was Sarah who got into their minds. She went into the terrible, dark places that most people feared.

And as for Gabe … his job was to work in the field. To take the knowledge that the team gave him. To find the missing. To work with his team and local law enforcement to close the cases.

And, of course, his job was also to finance the whole business.

Gabe gave a slow nod. "We've got a new case."

"Who does the blonde want us to find?" Wade pressed. "Hope it's not her husband." He gave a low whistle, one that had Gabe's eyes narrowing. "Because that woman was—"

"Off-limits," Gabe growled.

Wade's brows shot up.

"That woman," Gabe gritted out, "*is* the case." Then he pushed Eve's newspaper toward them. "She says her name is Eve Gray—no, actually," he corrected, "she doesn't *know* her real name. Eve is just the name she's using now." A name they'd given her in the hospital? He'd have to check on that.

"You're losing me, boss," Victoria said, even as she peered at the paper. "What does this 'maybe' Eve want us to do?"

"That story's about the Lady Killer case." Dean had stiffened. "The FBI's been tracking him for months. Ever since those bodies washed up after Hurricane Albert."

Hurricane Albert had been a vicious storm that struck early in the season, blasting across the southern Gulf Coast.

"We're going to find one of his victims? One that's still missing?" Victoria asked, then gave a low whistle. "Talk about high profile."

"We may have already found a victim." Gabe pointed to the black and white picture in the newspaper.

The room got very, very quiet.

"Eve doesn't remember anything before the third of June. According to her, she woke up in a hospital, with no memories whatsoever."

"Sarah needs to be here," Wade said, sitting a little straighter. "She could tell if the woman was faking or —"

"Eve Gray wants us to find out who she really is."

Frowning, Victoria glanced up at him. "What does your mystery blonde have to do with the Lady Killer?"

"One of the Lady Killer's suspected victims is Jessica Montgomery." Twenty-six. Blond. Green eyes. Five-foot-six. Last seen down on the Alabama Gulf Coast — on Dauphin Island. "And Jessica Montgomery happens to look *exactly* like Eve Gray."

"Define 'exactly,'" Dean said as he began to lean forward.

"A dead-on match." Gabe met Dean's eyes. He knew the ex-FBI agent would understand the importance of this case more than the others. Dean had worked plenty of serial cases during his time at the Bureau. He knew how hard it could be to stop a serial. How unlikely it was that a victim could survive an attack, but if a victim did survive …

"If that's her," Dean's voice was tight with tension, "then she could lead us to the Lady Killer. We could find him."

"And to the other missing victims," Victoria added, her fingers tapping on her chin. "She would have been at his kill scenes. She would have seen everything."

Seen everything and then blocked it all from her mind?

"*If* she's telling the truth," Wade threw out. Because Wade would be the suspicious one. Pretty face or not, Eve wouldn't just automatically be accepted by him. "You want me to start the check on her?"

Gabe nodded. "Tear into every detail of her time at St. Helen's Hospital. Rip into her life."

The new life that she had. The life that had begun just months ago.

The order was cruel, but it had to be done. Before they could start connecting any dots that might exist between Eve Gray and Jessica Montgomery, they had to find out as much information as they could about Eve's "recovery" at St. Helen's.

Gabe had seen enough families with broken hearts. He wasn't just going to call up the Montgomerys and tell them that their missing daughter had been found.

His team would investigate Eve. Tear into her life. Learn her every secret. If she checked out, *then* they'd move forward.

And for Eve, that would be the time when the real danger began.

I hope you're ready for what's coming. Because if she truly had escaped a killer once, she might not be willing to put herself in the target zone again.

But if she turned out to be Jessica Montgomery, there wouldn't be much of a choice for her. The media would find out about her survival. The FBI would rush in.

And the Lady Killer would know that she was still alive.

***

Eve woke, her heart racing in her chest and sweat covering her body. She grabbed the thin blanket and clutched it tightly in her hand. On the cots beside her, the other women kept sleeping. Soft snores filled the air. Faint mutters as Sue Smith talked in her sleep. Sue always talked, asleep or awake. Those mutters should have reassured Eve. *I'm not alone, others are here.*

Eve's gaze searched the darkness. She couldn't remember her dream, never could. But that was just normal … since she couldn't remember anything.

She rose from the cot, moving quickly. She always slept in her clothes. Sweatpants and a loose top. The men were down the hall, housed separately, but …

But they made her nervous. Most of them did, anyway. Just not Pauley.

She went to Pauley, because she knew that he'd be up, too. He never could sleep at night. He said the darkness reminded him too much of his time in battle.

She wasn't sure where or when Pauley had battled or even if he'd actually been in a war, but Eve never questioned him. He didn't question her story about having no past, so why should she question him?

Eve found him by the front door, in his usual guard position. He looked like a big dangerous shadow, but she knew he wouldn't hurt her. Pauley was gentle on the inside, good, but …damaged. She knew that, too.

He spoke slowly. Moved slowly.

It didn't matter. He was her friend.

"Someone's watching, Ms. Eve."

Pauley's quiet voice had her smiling at first, but then, as his words registered, her smile froze. "Wh-what do you mean?"

"I can feel the eyes. Just like I felt 'em in battle. The enemy's out there. He's watching."

She looked out of the window. Saw only streetlights. Darkness. "The doors are locked, right?" And they did have a security guard at the shelter. Except James spent most of his time sleeping. Pauley was a much better guard.

"Locked. Checked 'em all." Pauley rocked forward onto the balls of his feet. "Four times."

Her smile spread again. "Then I'm sure we're safe. Especially with you on duty." She said the words easily, but a chill still seemed to be icing her skin.

"Not safe. *Watching*." He put his hands against the door and leaned forward. "I should go patrol."

He was going to open the door. Go outside. "No!" The sharp order broke from her, and Eve wasn't sure why. She grabbed Pauley's big hand in hers and held tight. "Stand guard in here, with me."

He gave a hard shake of his bald head. "Need to patrol. *Patrol*."

But the darkness was scaring her. *Watching*. What if Pauley had seen someone out there?

Her left hand rose to her throat. Brushed lightly over the raised scar. A scream echoed in her mind. "Stay in here with me," Eve whispered.

Pauley glanced down at her, frowning.

She could confess to him, as she couldn't to anyone else. "I'm scared, Pauley," she said. Scared because she'd just taken a very dangerous step with her life. Eve Gray had no past. So she had no enemies. Nothing to fear.

But Jessica Montgomery? That woman had been a victim. She'd been hurt. Attacked. Left for dead?

The authorities were sure that Jessica Montgomery had been abducted by the Lady

Killer, a sadistic serial killer who was still on the loose. Still hunting.

Still looking for Jessica?

She knew her hand held too tightly to Pauley's arm. "Stay inside," she said again. It was too dark outside. And, like a child, she was very much afraid that …

Monsters waited in the dark.

***

BROKEN *will be available on 3/31/15.*
Thanks so much for checking out the excerpt!

A NOTE FROM THE AUTHOR

I hope you enjoyed reading NEED ME. I've had so much fun writing these characters. And, just because I've been getting emails about this particular guy...I wanted to say...Ethan *will* be getting a book of his own. His story will be out in late spring/early summer of 2015. I'm working on his book right now! He and Carly will get their turn for a novel in BEWARE OF ME.

Thank you for taking the time to read NEED ME. If you'd like to stay updated on my releases and sales, please join my newsletter list www.cynthiaeden.com/newsletter/. You can also check out my Facebook page www.facebook.com/cynthiaedenfanpage. I love to post giveaways over at Facebook!

Best,

Cynthia Eden

www.cynthiaeden.com

ABOUT THE AUTHOR

Award-winning author Cynthia Eden writes dark tales of paranormal romance and romantic suspense. She is a *New York Times, USA Today, Digital Book World,* and *IndieReader* best-seller. Cynthia is also a two-time finalist for the RITA® award (she was a finalist both in the romantic suspense category and in the paranormal romance category). Since she began writing full-time in 2005, Cynthia has written over fifty novels and novellas.

Cynthia is a southern girl who loves horror movies, chocolate, and happy endings. More information about Cynthia and her books may be found at: http://www.cynthiaeden.com or on her Facebook page at: http://www.facebook.com/cynthiaedenfanpage. Cynthia is also on Twitter at http://www.twitter.com/cynthiaeden.

HER WORKS

List of Cynthia Eden's romantic suspense titles:
- WATCH ME (Dark Obsession, Book 1)
- WANT ME (Dark Obsession, Book 2)
- NEED ME (Dark Obsession, Book 3)
- MINE TO TAKE (Mine, Book 1)
- MINE TO KEEP (Mine, Book 2)
- MINE TO HOLD (Mine, Book 3)
- MINE TO CRAVE (Mine, Book 4)
- MINE TO HAVE (Mine, Book 5)
- FIRST TASTE OF DARKNESS
- SINFUL SECRETS
- DIE FOR ME (For Me, Book 1)
- FEAR FOR ME (For Me, Book 2)
- SCREAM FOR ME (For Me, Book 3)
- DEADLY FEAR (Deadly, Book 1)
- DEADLY HEAT (Deadly, Book 2)
- DEADLY LIES (Deadly, Book 3)
- ALPHA ONE (Shadow Agents, Book 1)
- GUARDIAN RANGER (Shadow Agents, Book 2)
- SHARPSHOOTER (Shadow Agents, Book 3)

- GLITTER AND GUNFIRE (Shadow Agents, Book 4)
- UNDERCOVER CAPTOR (Shadow Agents, Book 5)
- THE GIRL NEXT DOOR (Shadow Agents, Book 6)
- EVIDENCE OF PASSION (Shadow Agents, Book 7)
- WAY OF THE SHADOWS (Shadow Agents, Book 8)

Paranormal romances by Cynthia Eden:
- BOUND BY BLOOD (Bound, Book 1)
- BOUND IN DARKNESS (Bound, Book 2)
- BOUND IN SIN (Bound, Book 3)
- BOUND BY THE NIGHT (Bound, Book 4)
- *FOREVER BOUND - An anthology containing: BOUND BY BLOOD, BOUND IN DARKNESS, BOUND IN SIN, AND BOUND BY THE NIGHT
- BOUND IN DEATH (Bound, Book 5)
- THE WOLF WITHIN (Purgatory, Book 1)
- MARKED BY THE VAMPIRE (Purgatory, Book 2)
- CHARMING THE BEAST (Purgatory, Book 3) - Available October 2014

Other paranormal romances by Cynthia Eden:
- A VAMPIRE'S CHRISTMAS CAROL
- BLEED FOR ME

`

- BURN FOR ME (Phoenix Fire, Book 1)
- ONCE BITTEN, TWICE BURNED (Phoenix Fire, Book 2)
- PLAYING WITH FIRE (Phoenix Fire, Book 3)
- ANGEL OF DARKNESS (Fallen, Book 1)
- ANGEL BETRAYED (Fallen, Book 2)
- ANGEL IN CHAINS (Fallen, Book 3)
- AVENGING ANGEL (Fallen, Book 4)
- IMMORTAL DANGER
- NEVER CRY WOLF
- A BIT OF BITE (Free Read!!)
- ETERNAL HUNTER (Night Watch, Book 1)
- I'LL BE SLAYING YOU (Night Watch, Book 2)
- ETERNAL FLAME (Night Watch, Book 3)
- HOTTER AFTER MIDNIGHT (Midnight, Book 1)
- MIDNIGHT SINS (Midnight, Book 2)
- MIDNIGHT'S MASTER (Midnight, Book 3)
- WHEN HE WAS BAD (anthology)
- EVERLASTING BAD BOYS (anthology)
- BELONG TO THE NIGHT (anthology)